MW01231533

Published in Great Britain by
L.R. Price Publications Ltd, 2023
27 Old Gloucester Street,
London,
WC1N 3AX
www.lrpricepublications.com

ISBN: 978-1-916613-10-2

Love in Lockdown

Based on Real Events

K. F. Fleming

CHAPTER ONE

**WEDNESDAY 25th MARCH 2020, EVE OF
LOCKDOWN, AUCKLAND CITY, NEW ZEALAND**

'Have you got a room?'

The girl standing in the lobby is tall with messy blond hair. The straps of her backpack frame her chest, creating a generous cleavage. She is smiling at me. She has a nice voice, a bit posh, but not too posh. She sounds British, from London, maybe.

I must admit, I hesitate while I take her in.

'There's a vacancy sign, and I've sent the taxi away,' she says. A bit bossy now.

I'm still hesitating. I have a lot on my mind.

'Course we have. Chelsea's not coming back. At least, it's not looking that way. Chelsea's old room: best in the house. Going to waste. If you're not going to let it, I'll move my stuff into it. It's a suntrap.'

This is from Frank, one of my lodgers. He's always poking his nose in where it doesn't belong. Old people, they really don't know what to do with themselves.

'I'm Frank,' he continues. 'This is an okay place. Just a pity about the landlord.' He laughs heartily and then splutters, working some phlegm into the back of his throat. It's not a welcome sound, especially when we are being warned not to cough over people.

1

'Meg.' The girl turns and smiles at Frank. She has a nice profile, an aquiline nose, aristocratic, but also friendly, not at all haughty. She turns back to me, unlatches her backpack and lowers it to the ground. Her breasts move around a lot during this manoeuvre, and I try not to look. 'So Chelsea's room then?' she says, raising a cute eyebrow at me.

'Um, yes, let me see. I think it's been cleaned,' I say, playing for time. It hasn't been cleaned professionally. I know this. I couldn't get anyone to come. The coronavirus has changed everything. No-one wanted to go anywhere, let alone clean up after a complete stranger. A lodging house is hardly a secure space. We're supposed to stay in our safe groups, family and close friends, people we can trust to do the right thing.

Not long after Chelsea took off, I had to do everything myself. My usual cleaning woman, Edith, said she had to protect herself. She had her family to think of, she said. The virus could be anywhere. It was the lurking, hidden enemy, and then she had terminated the conversation.

'You've left things late, Meg,' I say to the girl.

Meg. I need to remember her name. I'm not good at this, remembering people's names. 'Everyone's supposed to be settled by now,' I add.

'I know,' says Meg. 'Sometimes things don't go according to plan.' She is biting her bottom lip. She has full lips, a sort of Cupid bow, and a Lolita look. Actually, I've not read "Lolita", so I wouldn't know. But it's how I imagine Lolita would look: sexy and innocent at the same time.

'Just give me a minute,' I say, and I lift the key from the hook behind the counter. 'Take a seat. Frank will keep you company.' I point to the leather sofa by the front door.

I've always thought this was a nice touch: a sofa in a lobby: somewhere to sit, to be comfortable while the paperwork is being done or the cab is on its way, or a friend is visiting. It's what they have in the classier establishments.

Room One. It's been an unlucky room. It shouldn't be. It's at the front of the house with a view of the street. There's a big bay with high sash windows. "Sun-drenched, olde world charm with polished floors, pressed-steel ceilings and ornate fireplaces", was what the advertisement in the real estate magazine said. This is what caught my eye and made me buy this place. Room One has all of these features. I guess it was the reception room at one time, the parlour, the place where people in hats sipped tea in the morning and sherry in the evening as they sat upright in antimacassared wingback chairs. I put the key in the lock and push open the door. The room smells musty. I should have got rid of the rug. Those carpet-cleaning machines are not all they're cracked up to be. I flick open the brass stays and slide up the windows. At least they open. When I moved in, they were jammed shut with layers of paint. I check the floors. I spent hours scrubbing them, and they still smell of bleach and disinfectant. That Chelsea was a piece of work. Good riddance to her. What's that saying? Beauty is only skin-deep. Certainly true in her case. I leave the door open and return to the lobby. I hand Meg the key.

'Do you want to check it out first?' I ask.

'I'm good,' says Meg. 'Besides, I'm between a rock and a hard place. Midnight tonight and I've got to be tucked up somewhere.' She flicks her hair back in that flirty way of attractive girls and opens her mouth a little, so I can see the tip of her tongue.

'In that case,' I say, reaching out to shake her hand, 'welcome to Oak Tree Lodge. I'm Leo.'

'Oh, we can't do that anymore,' says Meg, and she bends her right arm and bumps her elbow onto mine and giggles. 'Hello, Leo,' she says and somehow manages to make the two words into something poetic. She draws out the first word and puts a lot of emphasis on the "o's". It makes me a bit dizzy.

I've always felt a bit off about the name Oak Tree Lodge. There isn't a tree anywhere near the place, let alone an oak. One day, I'll change the name to something like Murdoch Manor. Name it after me. It's got a ring to it.

I open up the bookings page on my computer and type in her name. Meg Hart. She makes a thing over the spelling. 'As in the deer,' she says, 'not the organ.' And then she asks me if I want her to spell it for me. I tell her no; I can manage. Then I ask how she would like to pay. She draws a wallet from the back pocket of her jeans and extracts a credit card. She hands it to me. It's a visa card. I slide it into my machine and take an imprint. I check the expiry date and hand it back to her. She folds her fingers around the card, but overreaches somehow, and I feel the warmth of her skin on mine.

'I need a shower,' she says. That hair flick again.

'Sure,' I say. 'The bathroom is at the end of the hall. I'll get you some towels. Just give me a minute.'

The linen cupboard is halfway up the stairs on the landing. I keep promising myself to find another storage area because I don't like people coming up the stairs. My apartment is on the second floor, and I value my privacy.

'Thanks,' she says, smiling at me. Meg has a slight speech impediment. It's not a lisp, but there is a fizz to her voice. Her tongue seems to get tangled in sibilants, so 'thanks' comes out as 'thanksh' as if there is too much saliva in her mouth. It's very charming.

I take the stairs two at a time and grab some soap and a couple of towels. I reach to the back of the shelf where I store the new ones. They are soft and fluffy, virginal. I hope she appreciates this. They're the latest colour, very fashionable, dove-grey with a red border. The shop assistant at Cranberry's picked them out for me. She was really helpful, a bit frumpy, and not all that attractive, but she more than made up for that. She offered me her phone number. I didn't know what to say. She wrote it down for me. I was going to throw it away. But I kept it. You just never know.

Frank is standing outside Room One when I come back down. He's wearing his hunting get-up today, not that he ever goes hunting. He seems to have only two outfits. Today it's corduroy trousers and a checked, woollen shirt. He has the look of someone queuing for a show, not quite loitering but definitely waiting for some action to brighten up his day.

'She's easy on the eye,' he says. 'Nice to have someone young here again. I miss that Chelsea.'

I knock on Meg's door, and she opens it a fraction and sticks her head out as if she is naked or something. I hold up the towels and soap.

'Perfect,' she says, grabbing them. She has to use both hands, and I see a lot of bare flesh. Her skin is pale, and she has some dark moles. This seems odd, the dark moles. Maybe she is not a natural blond. Girls, these days, what you see is never what you get.

I leave her to it. I'm the sort of landlord who lets everyone get on with things. I can't be checking on everything all the time. I expect my lodgers to act like grown-ups and not leave dishes in the sink or hair in the shower. Or the toilet unflushed. You would be amazed at how often people do their business and then walk out of a toilet as if the waste they have produced a second before has nothing whatsoever to do with them.

So I've gone to the considerable trouble of putting together some house rules. I've tried very hard not to cause offence. And I've kept it simple, something along the lines of leaving the space as you find it. Not that hard, is it? I've had this typed up, laminated, and posted in the service areas. With a message of thanks at the end, of course. Manners cost nothing. I've also supplied a house compendium like they do in top hotels with notes about local amenities and a map of the area. And bus times. People who come here never have their own car.

I decide on this occasion to do a quick reconnaissance. I start with the powder room: toilet lid down, plenty of loo paper. All good. And then the bathroom: shower wiped dry, basin scum-free and no dirty laundry lying on the floor. I can hear a dripping sound. I slide back the shower curtain. Panties dangle from the shower rose. Roz. They can't be anyone else's. I don't want an argument. Not today. Not with Meg here. I reach up, flick them off between my thumb and forefinger, and flush them down the toilet. Maybe Roz will be a bit more considerate in future.

I take a deep breath and make for the kitchen. Roz territory. Roz has been here for just over a year. She spends most of her time in the kitchen, which is strange because she never seems to eat anything. If asked, I would say she is borderline anorexic. She seems to live on coffee and cigarettes. And alcohol. House rules forbid smoking inside, so she is often in the garden. When I say garden, there is not much in the way of plants or trees. It's mainly concrete and outhouses, apart from a lush patch of grass close to the house. There's a laundry with its own entry, and next to that is a shed. I keep that locked. I've set up a washing line in the corner of the section. This doesn't attract morning sun, but from noon onwards, the drying is perfect, except in mid-winter.

Roz must be between cigarettes because she's in the kitchen. She has the newspaper laid out on the farmhouse-style dining table (it came with the house, along with the oak sideboard), and she's sitting in the captain's chair (her favourite), bent over the crossword puzzle.

'Impartial, thirteen letters,' she says without looking up.

'Dispassionate,' I say.

'Doesn't fit,' she says, taking a sip of coffee. Her mug is one of those personalised affairs. It has "Roz" in black lettering on its side, surrounded by red hearts and cupids with bows and arrows. It's a busy item. I suppose it's a good idea. To have your own mug, I mean. We're supposed to be social distancing.

'Disinterested, then,' I suggest.

She considers this and takes another sip of her coffee. She has thin hands with translucent skin. I can see the blue veins beneath. It's the only part of her on display. Roz wears jeans and long-sleeved tops in summer and winter.

'Yes,' she says and looks up at me. She grins and tucks a strand of hair into her rolled-up do. She writes in the letters. 'Chelsea come back?' she asks. 'No, it's someone new. Meg,' I say. 'Meg,' I repeat. I like saying her name. I hear the door to the bathroom open and close. And the key turns in the lock. Frank never bothers to lock the door. So it must be Meg. Sometimes I think Frank wants someone to walk in on him while he's at it. I can hear water running. The shower is running. Meg. Meg is taking a shower. I'm getting hot. I have to remember to breathe. Take it easy. Stay put. Don't go upstairs.

CHAPTER TWO

I'm upstairs. I'm in my apartment. Actually, I'm in my wardrobe. It's a walk-in, sort of. There is a rack at the front for my clothes and then a space behind fitted into the sloping ceiling. I can't stand up in here, exactly, but I can crouch or lie down. It's really very roomy. I spend quite a lot of time here when I'm in the mood. Right now, I'm in the mood. Meg has put me in the mood.

I've put earplugs in. I'm listening to music. Classical, not too heavy: Sibelius, gentle with a bit of a bounce to it. Those Finnish guys knew music. I guess they never got too hot. Or too cold.

I have things stored here. Some of it belongs to Chelsea. She left some stuff behind when she took off. It seemed silly to throw it away. A waste. I've got a pair of her shoes. Strange that she left these behind. You wouldn't think a girl would ever leave shoes behind. I found them under the bed. And a bra and panties, matching, black and lacy. They were under the bed as well. I guess she just didn't see them there. Chelsea was like that, careless and a bit chaotic. So I've got them too. I've laid them out on the floor next to the shoes: gold strappy things with high heels.

Chelsea was a bit of a lush. Don't get me wrong. She was nice enough, maybe a bit too nice, putting out and giving everyone the come-on. Flirty, that's what she was. She'd make you feel like a prince one minute and a frog the next. She liked to drink. White wine mainly:

chardonnay, sauvignon blanc, but also pinot gris—anything really. After a bottle of wine, she would come and sit on your knee and drape herself over you and make lewd suggestions. The next day, sober, she would have forgotten all about it. But, actually, I could tell she hadn't really forgotten about it. She would have that look about her, smug as if she knew more about you than your own mother. She really was a tease.

I've had to push my shirts aside to step through into this space. Now I take off some of my clothes and lay them on the floor. Just my jeans and underwear.

It gets hot in here, especially in summer. There are no windows and so, no ventilation, and it's a bit dark. But I'm ready to go. I crouch down and slide my wooden cover across. It conceals the peep-hole I've constructed on my wardrobe floor. I hope Meg doesn't like her showers super-hot. Too much steam and the glass gets fogged up. It's right over the top of the shower. I moved it there for safety after a near miss with Chelsea. I regret that now. I'm going to have a better steam extractor fan installed. I should have made the viewing hole way bigger. That would have given me a wider angle. But that's me: always erring on the side of caution.

I'm in luck. Meg hasn't got the hang of the shower. There isn't a mixer, so she has to fiddle with the hot and cold taps to get the temperature right. At the moment, she's standing outside the shower, reaching in, and adjusting first the hot tap and then the cold. Actually, the hot water in this place is set quite low. The perfect temperature for the shower needs no cold water at all. Meg will figure this out eventually.

I can see only her hands and part of her arms. She must be one of those girls who doesn't like to get her hair wet. She has nice hair, but, I must admit, it doesn't look styled. Not in that girly way, with kinks and ringlets and impossible shapes, a bit like Spaghetti Junction.

While I'm waiting, I drape Chelsea's panties over my groin. I don't put them on. That would be weird.

And now Meg is stepping into the shower. She is narrow and pale with slim hips. She reaches down and picks up the soap from the recess in the shower wall. I can see the shape of her back and waistline. Her shoulder blades stick out like little wings. But I notice she has a lot of tone — muscle even — especially in her arms. She has definition, biceps and triceps. She doesn't come across as a kick-arse kind of girl. Maybe she's just a gym bunny. I am wondering how anyone can be so pale at this time of year. We're at the tail end of an Indian summer. So where has she been? I must ask her. Politely. I don't want to come across as too interested. It's important to strike the right balance with lodgers. You can't be too familiar because then they think they can take advantage. Someone has to be the adult here. You would be amazed at how easy it is to get things wrong. Once someone thinks you're their friend, the next thing you know, they want to come up to your private apartment and look around or get a rent holiday or (and this is a complete no-no) store their stuff in the garden shed.

Meg is lathering the soap up between her hands under the nozzle, and the spray is heating up the room. I have only a minute or two left. Soon my viewing glass will be completely steamed up.

I wind Chelsea's bra around my haunches and clip it together. It's quite tight, a good feeling. Actually, it's more than good: it's heaven.

Meg is sliding her soapy hands up her neck. She has thrown her head back and is working on the foam. She has an elegant neck, long and delicate, a bit swan-like. And now she is moving down to her torso. She is cupping her breasts and sliding her hands underneath them. I am surprised at how fleshy they are when the rest of her is so tiny. But now I can't see her anymore. Too much steam. I really need to get that extractor fan installed. Tradespeople: they're not my favourite kind of people. They are more intent on snooping than getting anything done. It's lucky I'm a DIY kind of guy. I can do most things: unblock guttering, fix a fuse, repair a window, paint and putty.

But I don't do plumbing: too messy. Or electrics: too risky. I'll have to get someone in for the fan. I think I may have left it too late. With the lockdown, no-one wants to do anything. Essential services: that's all we're allowed. Is a bathroom fan an essential item? Maybe I'll make some calls. See what I can arrange.

I'm lying on my bed. The sight of Meg has made me want to take a shower and feel the tingle of water jetting onto my skin. But I know it will take too long. I always like to wash my hair properly when I have a shower. You know, shampoo it thoroughly and then apply conditioner.

And then dry it.

My hairdryer is playing up. It goes, but only at half throttle. So it takes twice as long. I've got quite a bit of hair, but there's a bald spot at the back, which I have to work on. It takes energy and finesse, and patience. So I'll do it later.

Instead, I try to relax. I spend a lot of time lying on my bed. It's a good place to be. I like my apartment. I've got all my artwork in my bedroom, away from the TV set. Art should be contemplated in silence, away from distractions. I've got Dali's Melting Clocks above my bed. There's quite a lot to that painting. Time passing, time distorting, reality and fantasy transcending each other. I thought long and hard about where to hang it. In the end, I thought the place of sleep, where so much time is spent, would be perfect. So there it is, above my four-poster.

I've also got Botticelli's Venus. I don't try to analyse this. I don't think, way back then, old Botti could have meant anything by it. I think he was just trying to capture the beauty of the female form. Those guys kept it simple. They didn't get bogged down with symbols and commentary and metaphysics. They were too into the here-and-now: the next hunk of cheese and canard and carafe of wine. It was all venal reality. This painting just wants us to look. I want to look right now — even though Venus looks nothing like Meg.

Just in case you think I'm a culture snob, I've got a Banksy print as well. I'm eclectic, see. It's one of his early ones. Girl with a Balloon. It's famous now. But I take some pride in getting in first. I didn't just climb on the bandwagon. That guy, he's sort of the opposite of culture. He likes to take the piss. But his pictures have something. They reach out: simple and stark. Yes, that's Banksy.

A bell is ringing in my sitting room. It's coming from downstairs. There's a repeater hooked into my sound system so that I know when someone comes in. I've got a visitor, someone looking for accommodation, no doubt. How can people be so disorganised? I forgot to take down the "Room Available" sign. And I didn't lock up. Meg. I blame her. Already I have let her into my head. Space. She's taking up space. And, actually, I know she's paid, but I haven't had a chance to spend any of it yet. Is that fair?

It's not someone looking for a room. I can tell that as soon as I come downstairs.

I'm a bit flustered because I've been in a rush to tidy myself up, but I can see that the guy in the lobby is on a mission. He has attitude. He's not exactly belligerent, but he's not laid-back, either. He's tall and well-built, wearing a suit, but he has taken off his jacket, and his shirt is stained with sweat, mainly under the arms. He smells a bit. But it's fresh, not old or putrid like the flavour around Frank sometimes.

'I'm looking for Chelsea,' he says.

'Leo Murdoch, mate, pleased to meet you,' I say.

'Yes, Chelsea mentioned you. You run this place?'

'I'm the owner, yes,' I say.

'Quentin Adams. I'm looking for Chelsea,' he repeats, looking down the hallway.

'She was here. But now she's not. She left two weeks ago.' I say. 'No forwarding address.'

'What, so she just went? Just like that?'

'Sorry, mate, that's all I can tell you.'

'Did she not say she was leaving?'

'No, she didn't, actually.'

'Did anything happen? You must have noticed something. People don't just up and leave, sneak out in the middle of the night without anyone noticing.'

'That's pretty much what happened. She was here for a couple of months, seemed happy enough, but

I didn't really know her very well. She was mostly out. And when she was here, she kept herself to herself.'

'That doesn't sound like Chelsea. She was everyone's friend. Warm and outgoing, always wanting to chat about anything and everything.'

Quentin has started to move down the hall towards the staircase.

'What's up there?' he asks, nodding towards the stairs.

'It's private. Not part of the guest quarters,' I say.

Quentin starts bouncing on his toes. He looks like an athlete waiting for the starter's gun, ready for a signal to bound up the stairs and have a look around.

I walk over to him. 'Look, I don't know what else to say. The police have been here. They've interviewed everyone, checked out the place.'

'Did they check the private quarters? I presume that's where you hang out.'

'They were very thorough,' I say, edging away from him towards the front door. 'Look, I'll let you know if we hear anything. Do you have a card?'

Quentin fishes out his wallet, a thin, fine-looking thing. Narrow, it gives the impression that Quentin lives in a cashless society. He draws a business card from a silky pouch and hands it to me. It's gold with black lettering. Flashy.

And then he is gone. The door whooshes as it closes on its pneumatic hinge. The sound lingers in the air.

'You should have mentioned Chelsea's cat.' Frank again. He's been listening. He's heard every word. For an old guy, he's got great hearing. He's standing in the doorway to his room, which is opposite Chelsea's old room.

I haven't mentioned this, but Chelsea left her cat behind. Prince. He's a beautiful cat, part Burmese, a smoky grey with white paws. I've grown attached to him, and he sleeps on my bed. Purrs a lot. I find that soothing. Frank is not very fond of Prince. And the feeling's mutual. Prince has let Frank know by signing off on his stuff from time to time. Usually his trainers. I call them trainers, but Frank never trains in them. He puts them on to go out to the letterbox or saunter down the street, which he does a lot. I often ask him where he goes. He's never very forthcoming.

But I have my theories.

One of the amazing drawcards of Oak Tree Lodge is its location. Amenities are important. People want to be able to walk to places. It's not exactly Vegas here, but there are cafés, restaurants, wine bars, second-hand shops, and, best of all, an arcade selling army memorabilia, rare books and sex toys. I think there's a massage parlour there as well. It's hard to know. The entranceway is unmarked and has a brass bell that you have to ring three times. So I've been told. I think Frank takes his ease around there, and who-knows-what lands on his trainers that might invite the attention of a male cat.

There's also a park. You can get to it by going through the arcade. It's not very big and has quite a slope. But there are wooden benches and phoenix palms, and a statue of Moses. It's really very pretty. During the day. At night it's a bit of a hang-out for undesirables.

I didn't mention Prince to Quentin because I didn't want him to decide that he needed to rescue him.

But also because it might appear weird that Chelsea would forget to take her cat.

K. F. FLEMING

CHAPTER THREE

Roz is in the kitchen. She's talking to herself.
'Tomorrow will be a new day. The dawn will come,' she is saying. This is the kind of language she uses these days. Biblical. As if life is a gift. We are navigating our way through streets of pestilence and peril, she often says. The coronavirus is everywhere, and we could be stricken at any time. We must stay home. Shelter in place. Choose your safe group and stay inside it. We're all to stay in our bubbles, which we have to respect. Stay home. Save Lives. On and on Roz goes, as if she's our PM.

There is a lot of talk about kindness. We must be kind to each other. Whole pages of the newspapers are devoted to this idea. It's all over the internet and Facebook. We mustn't be selfish. While we are being careful and staying home, we must also try to look out for each other. The news is full of stories of hysteria, reminiscent of wartime: people buying three gross of toilet rolls (I had to check that word: a gross amounts to one hundred and forty-four, apparently) and fighting over bottles of sanitiser. I must admit the word *bubble* was genius because the alternative is *leper colony*. That's what it's like. People avoid you in the street. They would rather move out onto the road and risk being run down than walk past you within six feet.

We are allowed to run errands that are defined as essential. Trips to the supermarket are sanctioned. There you can get everything, pretty much. Meat, groceries, fresh vegetables and liquor. There's plenty of liquor available, I've noticed.

And so has Roz because she's brought back a whole lot of it. It's in a carton in the corner of the kitchen. And she's also purchased groceries, which she is unpacking and sanitising.

Right now, she's washing the lettuce.

She has filled the sink with soapy water, and the pink bucket from the laundry is set up on the bench top. She is tearing the leaves off a cos, swirling them in the sink, and then dipping them in the bucket. The dish rack is full of tomatoes and apples, and avocados. And maybe peaches; it's hard to tell. Everything looks different when it's sopping wet. Roz is laying the lettuce leaves on top. A warm breeze wafts through the kitchen window over this pile of laundered produce.

There is a box on the floor that seems to be full of baking and breakfast stuff: flour, oats, muesli, rice, bread, biscuits and other things which weren't on my list. Roz is hoisting it onto the bench and extracting each item for inspection. It's as if she has never seen a bag of flour before. She's got everything out now, and she's holding her hands up high. She has vinyl gloves on and looks a bit like a surgeon who has just scrubbed up, ready to perform life-saving surgery. Her brow is furrowed as she picks up the flour and squints at the label. She's short-sighted even with her glasses on. Especially with her glasses on. Roz has those cheap jobs from the shop along the road. Number ones. She's had these for as long as I've known her, and they are not really up to the task.

'Hey, you got the mixed nuts,' I say, scooping up the plastic zip-lock from the counter.

'I haven't washed that,' says Roz.

'I'll risk it,' I say, peeling open the top and popping a pecan.

'Have you ever considered how nuts are harvested?' asks Roz. 'I mean, they're probably hand-picked, hand-shelled.'

I'm mid-chew and trying to think of an answer. I don't want Roz insisting on washing them. I like nuts salted; otherwise, what is the point? I don't want to get her started. Roz is borderline hysteric and definitely at the upper end of the OCD spectrum.

'These nuts were picked off trees way before Covid-19 was even thought of. But just to be sure, I'll dispose of them,' I say, putting them in my shirt pocket.

Roz seems satisfied with this. She's unscrewing the top of a bottle of hand sanitiser and dispensing a good dollop onto her gloves. She's rubbing her hands together and then wiping the bottle. She repeats the exercise with a second bottle.

'Here,' she says, handing the sanitiser to me, 'put this at reception. I'll leave the other one here.'

I take the bottle and get ready for her next pronouncement.

'We only get one chance at this,' she says. Roz talks about single chances a lot. I wonder if she made an epic mistake at some point in her life. Maybe Mr Right was right in front of her, and she wasn't paying attention. Maybe she hadn't washed her hair that morning or wasn't wearing the right shoes. I notice she shampoos her hair every day here and is fastidious about pinning it up. It's not very flattering. It's too neat. It reminds me of my history teacher: prissy and closed-up. Sometimes messy hair can be very sexy. It screams abandonment and the exact opposite of closed-up.

It suits Meg.

'Right,' I say.

'I hope that new girl is going to fit in,' says Roz with a sniff.

'You haven't met her.'

'I know, but what sort of girl has nowhere to go?' Roz is wiping down a box of Weetabix. She floats the cloth in the sink when she's finished and wrings it out.

'I don't know, but she seems okay. She's got a nice voice,' I say.

'So did Myra Hindley,' says Roz.

She's got me there. I've no idea how Myra Hindley spoke. But I know who she was. She was a serial child killer. She was known as The Moors Murderer, along with Ian Brady. I let it go. The last thing I want to talk about is murder.

Roz is intent on the cardboard box of washing powder. She obviously doesn't want to get it wet.

'I think I read somewhere that shiny surfaces are the ones to look out for, you know, glass and plastic and bench tops. But cardboard and paper are okay after seventy-two hours,' says Roz. She has rinsed her hands in the bucket and is drying them off. She has forgotten to roll back the sleeves of her shirt, and she has soap around her wrists. She keeps trying to push her cuffs up by rubbing them against her cheeks so she has suds on her chin. 'What do you say we just store the boxes with the dry goods and wine out in the shed?' she suggests.

'The shed is locked,' I tell her.

'You must have the key,' she says. 'I need somewhere to store the wine. Glass can be a carrier, you know, of the coronavirus. I can't be washing all the bottles individually.'

'I haven't opened the shed for years. I'll have to try to locate the key,' I say.

Actually, I know exactly where the key is. I've got it upstairs, in a safe place. I don't use the shed a lot. But it's private. It's got stuff in it that I don't want other people sniffing around. When I do visit, I make sure everyone's out. Privacy, it's important, as I think I've mentioned. Other people think they own you, especially in a boarding house situation. They think you're their mate and want to know every little thing about you. What they don't understand is that life is a business arrangement. Everything comes down to money in the end. Roz and Frank are here because they pay to be here. I call them guests of Oak Tree Lodge. But they're paying guests, here because they hand over their credit cards every month.

That Chelsea girl, I would probably have given her a discount. You know, come to an arrangement of some kind. If she'd been more accommodating, I'd have returned the compliment. But she wasn't, and I didn't.

'Well, maybe you could have a hunt for it and let me know. This is a situation where we all need to step up. The Prime Minister has said lockdown is for at least four weeks,' says Roz, manoeuvering the box of groceries into the corner by her case of wine. And now she is taking off her gloves and dropping them into the waste bin.

I've put a whiteboard up in the living area. It's wall-mounted next to the dresser. I despise the look of it. It's plastic and modern and unclassy, very out-of-place at Oak Tree Lodge, where everything is Edwardian. Builders were more than tradespeople in those days. They were artisans who took pride in their work and used only the best materials. The skirting boards are wide and fluted with rosette architraves to match. The ceilings are solid timber, tongue-and-groove, no nails required. They knew how to do things a hundred years ago. The best thing about the architecture is the fireplaces. There's one in every bedroom: cast iron registers with tiles depicting tulips and colourful birds. The one in the front room, Chelsea's old room, is very fancy with a wooden surround featuring carved corbels. Of course, I never use them. There are by-laws forbidding fires in the city, but I keep the chimneys swept.

I often think about the first day I saw Oak Tree Lodge. There were a lot of things I didn't notice. I was so taken by the feel of the place, its sheer history and drama, that I failed to pick up on the deferred maintenance. I've already mentioned the jammed windows. The truly big thing was the old-fashioned wall construction. There was no such thing as gib in those days. The walls were made of boards and scrim. And then wallpaper was glued on top, the busier the better.

So my first job was to cover all this. Even then, the surface was pretty uneven, so I had it plastered. A paint finish was what the plasterer promised. And he delivered. When it came time for painting, I felt I had to be careful with the colour. Everyone had a suggestion. Passers-by used to walk in and offer their two-pennies' worth. Paint it white; you can't go wrong, many said. A different colour for every room, others said. On and on with the well-meaning advice. Of course, I ignored everyone.

I hired an interior designer. Amanda was very imposing. She swept into the house in her high heels, which I insisted she remove, and went from room to room with her oversized lips and bird-like eyes. And then she took a palette of paint colours from her bag and walked through the house again with her head on one side, and her lips clamped together. This took the whole morning. I shut the front door and went down the road for a coffee.

'Antique Yellow for the hallway and front rooms,' she announced when I returned.

'Uh, huh,' I said.

'I know it takes guts to think outside the box,' she said.

I took her advice. It was all a long time ago. But I have no regrets. Timeless, that's what it is. And sophisticated. Sage green for the kitchen/living area. It has just the right amount of drama and energy, she said. It's soothing and invigorating at the same time. And it brings the outdoors in and makes your living space part of your garden. And Old Yellow for the hallway and bedrooms. It's warm and subtle in perfect harmony. You have a lot going on in the fireplaces and ceilings, and you don't want to take anything away from that. At least, I think that's what she said. I wasn't really listening too carefully. Those clamped lips were quite a distraction.

I just wish I had kept a note of the paint formulas. When I had to repaint Chelsea's room, I couldn't get a perfect match. The yellow is too brassy. It doesn't have that subtle parchment look.

Getting back to the whiteboard. It's been necessary, a way of communicating. Initially, I was the only one to post messages, things like "dishes in the sink", "hob", or "someone owes rent". I always took care not to point fingers. I try not to undermine anyone. People have to sort themselves out.

Roz is wiping the board down with a cloth, and she is writing something in her sloping, cursive scrawl. She likes to think she's an artist. Actually, she's a retired hairdresser. Next to the word "biscuits", she's drawn some cat whiskers.

She's obviously forgotten to get food for Prince.

'Have you locked reception up?' she suddenly asks.

'Official lockdown doesn't begin until 11:59 pm,' I say.

'Maybe not, but the virus is out there. It's everywhere. People are infected. We've got one hundred and fifty-five cases. Forty-four new cases yesterday. It's not like in the fairy tale where everything turns into something else at midnight,' says Roz. 'And, besides, we're full now. We shouldn't have let that stranger in.' Roz is glaring at me.

I really want to change the subject. Actually, I don't want to change the subject in my head, just with Roz. I want her to go outside and have her fix, leave me to check out Meg. Where is she? I need to talk to her and see her with her clothes back on so that I can concentrate on normal things.

And now the front door is banging closed. Someone has walked in.

And Roz is screaming.

CHAPTER FOUR

I've not mentioned Julius. He stays here too. That's unless he's at his girlfriend's, which is most of the time. He's a student. He wants to be a writer. He's studying journalism at the University. That's not really writing, I suppose. He'll be just recording the facts. It amazes me that anyone could spend three years being shown how to write facts. Although, when I think about it, half the stuff you read in the news these days is made-up. Fake news, they call it. Julius will be perfect for the job. He has an overactive imagination and a temper to match.

Right now, he looks as if he's about to blow.

He walks straight past me through the hallway and into the kitchen.

'Good to see you, too,' I say as I follow him.

He's standing by the whiteboard, checking for messages. Sometimes people ring on the landline for Julius, and we are asked to pass something on. Weird when everyone has an iPhone and can interface on Messenger, Skype, Facetime, and Zoom (whatever that is), and God-knows-what else; it's hard to keep up. Why not just send a text and wait, I often think. Wouldn't that be polite? You know, give the recipient a minute to work out a strategy?

'Jesus, Julius, why aren't you on Waiheke at the vineyard? Where's Poppy?' I ask.

'Well, you know what, I had a good think, you know, some deep soul searching, and I decided that there was no place I'd rather be than right here with my best buddies,' he says grimly.

'You have to be kidding. Waiheke Island's got to be the safest place in the whole world, surrounded by water, and not a single case reported,' I say.

'Did you have a fight with Poppy?' asks Roz. She's settled herself at the dining table, ready for the excitement of someone else's misfortune. She's got over her terror. Adrenaline has been replaced by morbid curiosity.

Julius has his phone out and is staring at the screen. His face is screwed up, and his mouth is open, and not in a friendly way.

'Yes, you did have a fight with Poppy,' says Roz with satisfaction.

'She's a selfish bitch,' says Julius.

'What did you do?' asks Roz.

'What did I do?'

'Yes.'

Julius is a little on the short side (a bit taller than me, if I'm honest) and wiry. He drops into a dining chair and stretches himself out in the way that short guys do. He has rather a large head with a lot of hair, which I quite envy.

'I didn't do anything,' he says.

'Okay,' says Roz, elongating the second syllable.

Julius is punching stuff into the screen. It's as if he's in a boxing match. He's intent, focused and extremely tense.

'If you must know, I wrote an article. It was an assignment. It's not as if I had a choice. I had to do it for Uni. Choose an aspect of what is happening in Auckland society at the moment, with Covid-19 as its theme, and write two thousand words. Make it interesting. Get the human-interest angle. A whole lot of stats won't make the cut. So that's what I did. Oh, God.' He leans back in his chair and crosses and uncrosses his ankles. Julius does this sort of thing a lot. Body rearrangements. They reflect his mood. Right now, he's trying to extricate himself from the deep shit he's in.

'So what happened?' asks Roz. She is now leaning across the table towards Julius with her hands outstretched. Her face is lit up.

'Well, just to get feedback before I submitted my piece, you know, to get another view, I shared it with one of my mates in the course, who shared it with another of our mates, who shared it ...' Julius pauses to rub his jaw. He has a big jaw, Brad Pittian, if you like that sort of thing.

'And the rest is history,' I say.

'You could put it like that,' says Julius. He's now rubbing his right temple. 'Well, so Poppy got hold of it.'

'And she didn't like it?' I say. 'What, too many spelling mistakes and infelicitous turns of phrase?'

I can be like this, not as empathetic as I should be. Julius is such a pedantic prig, always correcting me. I can't resist.

'Nothing like that,' says Julius more to himself than me. 'No, I chose as my topic, The Effect of Covid-19 in Primary Schools.'

'A noble and important study,' I say, trying to lift my game. 'But you mentioned Poppy, right? She's a teacher. You made it personal. You made it about her.'

'That's what you're supposed to do. Make it relatable. People want the facts, sure, but they also want the human element.'

'But you went too far.' This is from Roz. She has moved back from the table and is sitting bolt upright with her arms folded.

'So I go back to my original question. You could be frolicking as free as a faun' (I like to show off my literary side around Julius) 'in your parents' vineyard, plucking grapes and tasting wine. Why aren't you? And haven't your olds got a swimming pool?'

'I have to make things right with Poppy,' says Julius miserably.

'Well, it's too late now,' says Roz. She has unfolded her arms and is leaning forward again. A strand of hair has escaped her up-do, and she's trying to anchor it back in place. 'You're here, and she's there, wherever there is. That's it. For four weeks. Minimum.'

Julius is on his phone again.

'And since you're here, we might as well start off the way we mean to go on. Anyone who leaves the lodge on an essential errand' (Roz puts air quotes with her index fingers around the word, *essential*) 'must take their temperature when they get back.' And with that, Roz reaches under the table and produces a pistol-shaped device.

'What the fuck is that?' says Julius.

'It's what's going to keep us all safe,' says Roz.

'Uh, huh,' says Julius, turning back to his phone.

'It's for taking our temperature, monitoring things.' Roz has raised her voice a little. 'And we need to take the new girl's temperature, make sure she's okay.'

'Where did you get it?' I ask, without wanting to know the answer.

'Look, I got it because it's contactless. They use them at airports. You just point it at your forehead, and it buzzes if you've got a fever. We all need to use it daily. At least once a day,' says Roz, laying the gauge on the table in front of Julius.

And then his phone rings. Julius answers it, a hopeful expression on his face.

'I didn't lie to you,' he says urgently and immediately. Poppy likes to get down to business, no time for pleasantries. I've noticed this. A quality in a girl. Julius should be more appreciative. He tucks the phone between his shoulder and ear and navigates his way through the screen door. It's very hot today, so I've got the back door open. Roz is following his every move. She has that look about her: as if she has got to the shower scene in "Psycho" and there's a power outage. She grabs her cigarettes, pours herself a glass of wine to-go and follows him into the garden.

'What do you mean, by omission?' shouts Julius. He really has got very strident. I've noticed how people talk way more loudly when they're on their phones — like by about ten decibels. Julius is no exception.

'Of course, you can trust me,' he says. He's not standing still. He's walking in circles around the garden.

'I do have my own ideas. What do you mean?' Louder now.

'It wasn't that personal,' he wheedles. The circles he is inscribing on my lawn are getting smaller, I can't help noting. I'm standing by the kitchen windows, which afford a perfect view over the backyard.

'It put you in a good light.' Quiet now. A long pause.

'Well, I think it did.' And then Julius adds, 'And so did everyone else.' I'm thinking this last bit won't be going down well. This is red-rag material. Pointing out that Julius's article is all over the internet. I am proved right because Julius is now holding the phone away from his ear.

'Well, what is the point then?' he finally asks. His voice has lifted an octave, and he has run out of lawn, a bit like his argument.

'Christ, Poppy, we're in the middle of a global pandemic, and you're making this all about you. You know what,' he continues, but he doesn't finish the sentence. Poppy has clearly had enough of his cowardly excuses. Why doesn't he just man up and apologise? I would have terminated the conversation ages ago, and I would definitely have hung up at once on anyone who uses the phrase "global pandemic". How can a pandemic be anything other than global? I hope to hell Julius is never let loose on any self-respecting journalism outlet. There's enough media drivel out there without having to read the miserable outpourings of Julius Swann.

Roz is nodding and taking a sip of her wine. She's in her comfy place. In the garden with her favourite companions: wine and weed. Of course, the floor show is a welcome addition. She's had a wicker rocking chair delivered. She bought it on Trade Me and spray-painted it: British racing green. And then she filched a cushion from the couch in the living room and patted it into place on the slats of the seat. I let it go. It's a nice look, actually — fits the vibe of the house. Roz keeps saying it reminds her of Boston. She's been to Boston, apparently. She's leaning back and rocking herself gently.

'The hydrangeas and wicker and return verandas in Boston, it's all so cheerful and real,' she often says, usually after a couple of wines. Roz is always talking about things being real. Sometimes I think it's because she feels the exact opposite. She likes to feed the sparrows in the yard tiny bread fragments. I guess it's transactional. Birds scampering and scrapping and tweeting over food is something real. Roz is making things happen. In her world, anyway.

So this is a taste of things to come. Life at the lodge in lockdown. Does Roz need to go, I am wondering. We've got four weeks of this. There's a blowfly batting at the windows above the sink bench. Roz is a greenie. She likes to recycle. She's set up compost at the back of the garden. Admirable, really, except for the maggots and the flies that come with it. I look around for the fly swat. Fly-spray is banned. By Roz. I'm mid-swat when I hear a footfall.

CHAPTER FIVE

'Oh, hello,' I say. Meg has walked into the room, and I am finding it difficult to breathe.

She is a picture of loveliness, casual but glamorous at the same time.

'Hello to you too,' she says. There are lots of "o"s in this sentence, and Meg has opened her mouth wide to frame the words. Her lips form a perfect circle. I have to look away.

'How was the shower?' I ask.

'Divine. Just what I needed,' says Meg. She grabs her hair and pulls it back and up as if she is going to fasten it into a ponytail. As she does this, her dress comes up a bit, showing her thighs. They're a part I couldn't see when she was in the shower. Lovely, lots of definition, but not too much. Girls shouldn't be overly ripped. It's not feminine.

'I can't thank you enough for letting me in, you know. Scary times and you were all settled, ready to batten down the hatches in your safe bubble, and I crash in.' Meg walks over to me by the window. She takes the swat from me and brings it down on the fly buzzing at the glass in a lightning-fast rap.

'Wow!' I say.

'I play badminton,' she says, laughing and handing back the swat.

'So do I,' I say. I don't know why I say this. I've never played any racquet sports, not even ping-pong, although I think I could have aced that. How hard can it be?

'We should have a game sometime. You know when we can,' says Meg. A strap of her dress has slipped down over her shoulder, and she is taking her time to pull it back up. She is looking hard at me as she does this as if daring me to look at her bare shoulder, which is very pale against the black of her dress.

'I would like that,' I say.

'It's a date then.' When Meg smiles, her nose takes part somehow. Little wrinkles appear on its bridge.

'It's a date,' I echo. And Meg is doing that elbow bump thing again. She really is very friendly.

'Oh, look, you've got a garden,' she says, leaning over the bench and looking out. 'Lucky me that I came here. I love the outdoors. I love walking, exploring.'

'Where are you from? You sound a bit, I don't know…,' I say. Of course, I want to know all about Meg, but at the same time, I don't want to be uncool.

'I'm from London,' says Meg, turning back to me. 'I came here to experience the great outdoors.' She shrugs. 'So far, I've visited my uncle in Rotorua, did a few walking tracks. Heaven. And I was heading north, Bay of Islands.'

'It'll keep,' I say.

'Hey, I've got some wine. I didn't have a chance to get food, but I've got some champagne. Let's have a drink, a toast to Oak Tree Lodge and all who sail in her,' says Meg. That nose wrinkle again. Before I can say anything, she races up the hallway.

I'm not a drinker. I'm not exactly teetotal, but I find it hard to concentrate after a few wines. Or beers. I like to be in control. I know what can happen when you let your guard down. I can't afford to do that. But maybe I'll make an exception for Meg.

'Here,' says Meg, giggling as she flies into the room. She's a bit breathless. Not that fit, then. She's thrusting a bottle into my hands. It's not chilled, but I really don't want to pass up this opportunity to drink champagne with her. I tear off the top and ease out the cork. 'Do we have flutes?' she asks. She perches lightly on the captain's chair at the end of the dining table and crosses one leg over the other. She is wearing chunky white sneakers, which make her ankles look delicate.

'Sure,' I say, and I reach into the glass cabinet and grab two from the top shelf. I can't believe my luck. Here I am in lockdown with the sexiest girl in the world. The only downside is my other guests—Julius especially. Maybe he'll make it up with Poppy and piss off.

'So here's to it,' says Meg. She takes the glass I have filled and chinks it to mine.

'How come you've got this place? You seem too young to own anything this grand.'

'Oh, you know, right place, right time,' I say. I take my time coming out with this. I have a sip of champagne first. And then I add, 'My parents died in a car crash and left me everything. I don't tell many people this. For one thing, it's sad, and I don't want sympathy.'

Actually, I am hoping this will put my stocks up with Meg and make her feel sorry for me. And impressed that I picked myself up and got on with things as real men do. This doesn't always work. I told this story to a girl once, and I never saw her again. She just thought I was a loser.

'I wish I could be in the right place at the right time,' says Meg with a laugh. 'I'm exactly the opposite.

Look at me: doing my O.E. in the midst of the scariest shit the world has ever seen.'

And then she catches herself. 'But, you know what, if not for Covid-19, I would never have met you. So ...'

She doesn't finish the sentence. But she is raising her right eyebrow. And she is flashing her teeth, and her tongue is somehow visible. I finish the sentence for her.

'You would never have met me, right?' I say. It feels nice to put the words "you" and "me" into the same sentence.

Meg gets it because she's nodding and flicking back her hair and fiddling with the strap of her dress.

And now Julius is coming back inside from the garden. He's taken his shirt off, and he's got his usual bullshit tee-shirt on underneath. They're always black affairs with pithy sayings printed on the front. Actually, they're the opposite of pithy. They're a turn-off. He thinks they make him look like an intellectual, but actually, they just make him look like a prize arsehole. Today, it's not even English: "Vera, Modo". It must be Italian or something. I try not to look, and I certainly never ask Julius what his logos mean. I don't want to give him the satisfaction.

'Why, hello, I'm Meg,' says Meg, treating Julius to her killer smile. Without getting up, she extends the crook of her elbow. But not full-on: she's hanging back with it a bit, I'm pleased to note.

'Julius, I'm Julius.' He's bumping his right elbow to hers. 'Where did you spring from?'

'I'm the new lodger,' says Meg.

'Staying long?' asks Julius. 'I guess that was a pretty stupid question. No-one knows. It all depends on King Covid, right? Must be tough. Can't really plan ahead too much.' Julius has parked himself at the dining table next to Meg and is leaning in close.

Meg takes a sip of her champagne. Her lips make love to the rim of her flute. She has a way of doing things that is very sensual. It's very hot in the room, even with the door open, and I'm beginning to sweat. I can feel a trickle down my back.

'It's really okay. I feel blessed to be here, you know, amongst real people. Kiwi people.'

'You think?' says Julius.

'I don't like hotels. They're so impersonal. What's the point of travel if you don't get to meet the locals? You know, mix it up a bit. Hey, do you want some champagne? Leo and I are celebrating.'

I like Meg saying this as if we're an item. But, at the same time, she's giving him an opening to gate-crash our gig.

'How's Poppy?' I ask.

'I've got a beer,' says Julius, going to the fridge and ignoring me.

I should explain we've got two fridges, one for food and the other for drinks. Roz calls the drinks fridge her Bar Bitch. It belongs to her. She had it delivered shortly after she came here, about a year ago. It is bigger than the main fridge with shelving for bottles and trays for cans. It's out of place here, but I felt I had to give in. I've got it in the corner away from the dresser, so it's not too imposing. Roz makes sure it's always fully stocked.

'Hey, love your shirt,' says Meg.

'I'm a writer, a journalist,' says Julius. He tucks his chin in and looks down at the writing on his tee-shirt as if seeing it for the first time.

'Vera modo. Nothing but the truth,' says Meg.

'Principles first. So much bullshit in the media. I admire

you for that.' Meg is giving Julius a look that could easily be misinterpreted. She needs to watch that.

Julius flips the cap off his beer and takes a swig. 'That's me; what you see is what you get. The plain unvarnished truth,' he says.

I am wondering what Poppy would have to say about that. No wonder she dumped him. What took her so long?

'Hey, that's impressive,' says Meg. 'Have you had a scoop yet? Any Pulitzers in the wings?'

'This is my first year, so, no,' says Julius. He says this as if he's fully expecting a golden writing gong in year two. 'So far, we're concentrating on ethics, you know, rooting out the truth and telling it how it is. Facts first, that's our motto.'

'How long was that lecture?' I ask. I'm thinking it would take about ten seconds to fully explore and nail that premise. If that.

Julius doesn't always respond to my questions. Especially when he knows I'm not really interested in the answer.

'And we've been studying "In Cold Blood" by Truman Capote. It's the best piece of creative non-fiction ever written.'

'Is that what you were doing in your latest assignment, the one about Poppy? Writing made-up truth?' I ask. This must be another of those questions because Julius doesn't trouble himself to answer.

'So you've got Chelsea's old room,' he says.

'I guess,' says Meg.

'It's a great room,' says Julius. 'The best in the house. Just a bit unlucky.'

'Oh?'

'People don't stay long there.'

'What happened to Chelsea?'

'That's the thing. No-one seems to know,' says Julius.

'Not even her boyfriend,' says Meg. 'Was that her boyfriend who called earlier?' She addresses this question to me.

'Yes, that was her boyfriend. Quentin,' I say, 'He doesn't seem to get it. It would never occur to him that maybe Chelsea left suddenly for a reason.'

'He seemed really upset,' says Meg. 'And a bit suspicious, I must say.' How does she know all this, I'm wondering. She must have been listening at her door, eavesdropping.

I top up Meg's glass. I'm careful to tilt it properly so that the champagne doesn't foam up. I know how to do things, and I want to impress her. I also want to change the subject.

'She's only been gone for two weeks,' I say. 'She probably just wanted to get away for a bit.'

'People normally say goodbye when they leave places,' says Julius.

'She was a bit down,' I say. 'Sometimes saying goodbye is the hardest thing of all.'

'Yes, I know what you mean,' says Meg. 'It's like trying to leave a boring dinner party early. The other guests feel insulted. They insist you stay only because that makes them feel better, less tedious and mind-numbing. If you walk out on them, they take it personally.'

This girl is smart. She has a brain. And a heart. I can't wait to get her alone so we can have a proper conversation about important things. Art, for instance, and architecture. And sex. And maybe books. I'll have to bone up because, I have to admit, I don't read all that much.

'How do you know so much about her, Leo?' asks Julius, destroying the moment.

'She missed out on the part she was auditioning for. You know, in that play,' I say.

Chelsea was an aspiring actress, but she had zero prospects. No-one had ever asked her to even try for a part, except this one time. But I really want to talk about something else. I'm hoping this will close down the conversation. It's starting to feel a bit forensic around here as if Chelsea's the victim of foul play, and Oak Tree Lodge is the scene of the crime.

Meg takes a chug of champagne and tucks her feet under her. I am treated to a glimpse up her dress as she rearranges herself. Julius, who is sitting beside her, misses this. The show has been put on especially for me. Meg is giving me so many signals. And she knows I'm picking up on them. She has red panties on. My scalp is starting to itch. I have a slight case of seborrhoea, mostly at the hairline—which is what Meg is staring at right now. I've run out of Nizoral and am having to make do with ordinary shampoo. It's not working. I resist the temptation to scratch.

'What an interesting girl this Chelsea must have been,' says Meg. 'What was her surname? Would I recognise it? Did she get lots of interesting parts?'

'Green, her name was Chelsea Green,' I say. 'And no, she didn't, not to my knowledge anyway. Maybe in another life. She was only here two months.'

There is fussing and banging at the back door. Prince. He is trying to get in through the cat flap. Someone has locked it. Frank. He's always trying to keep Prince out of the house. I walk over and flip it open, and a ball of grey fur leaps through and darts down the hallway.

CHAPTER SIX

'Hello, I'm Roz.' Roz has come inside and is standing by the back door. She's addressing Meg, but she's social distancing. She looks scared. She's holding her empty wine glass in her right hand and hugging her waist with her left as if she's trying to ward something off.

Meg chooses this moment to sneeze. Fortunately, she's up on Covid-19 etiquette and manages to bring her elbow up to her face in good time.

'Oh, my God!' wails Roz.

'It's okay, it really is. I'm just a bit allergic to animals, cats mainly,' says Meg. 'I'm Meg; so happy to meet you. So happy to be here. I can't thank you enough.'

Roz likes to be thanked, especially when she has done nothing to deserve it.

'Would you like a glass of champagne?' says Meg, pointing to the near-empty bottle.

Roz marches to the dining table, seizes the bottle, and takes it to the sink. She turns the faucets to full and rinses the bottle. She then wipes it with the dish cloth and hands it to me. Finally, she squirts some sanitiser onto her hands and rubs it in vigorously. She has watched way too much "Grey's Anatomy", I'm thinking. And then, she picks up the thermometer and holds it to Meg's forehead. She's obviously done this before. She pulls it away and checks the screen. She looks satisfied.

'That would be lovely,' she says finally. 'I'm okay with my regular wine glass,' she adds, holding it out. I pour her half a glass. There's not much left, and I want to top up Meg later. 'Thank you,' says Roz with just the right tone to suggest she is doing everyone a favour.

'Did you know,' says Roz to no-one in particular, 'that the average diameter of the coronavirus is one hundred and twenty nanometres?'

'That's small, right?' says Meg.

'A human hair is about seventy-six thousand. Nanometres that is. So yeah, you could say that,' replies Roz. She is rubbing her right finger around the rim of her glass. 'The point being that it is completely invisible to the naked eye, which means we have to be hyper-vigilant. How long are you staying?'

'No real plans. It's hard to know. I guess I'm here for as long as it takes. At least during lockdown, and that's a month, so we'll see.' Meg is smiling at Roz, but I can see that it's an effort. I don't blame her.

'Anyway, you're here for dinner,' says Roz, pursing her lips.

'Of course,' I say, maybe a bit too quickly. I don't usually eat with my guests. I have my own kitchen, and I prefer to keep some stuff private. Sharing food is definitely intimate. It's a ritual, almost a dance. It's how most relationships begin if you think about it: date-night at a restaurant. It gives you an opportunity to find out quite a lot about someone, how they eat, how much they eat, and what they eat. This last one is probably the most important of all. There's so much prissy nonsense these days about vegetarians, vegans, pescatarians, fruitarians; you name it. The one that kills me is the flexitarian. These people make a virtue out of eating absolutely everything, even offal and quail. And bats' brains, when they can get them. That's what the flexi part of the word indicates. I think these reckless eaters, who have no scruples at all, are probably half the reason the world is beset by Covid-19. I read something on the internet about this. I actually hate the internet. It's so tomorrow. Who needs it? I'm very comfortable with what happened today, yesterday, last week, and last month. I could go on. I'll be making an exception tonight to my eating-alone rule. I really want to spend some more time with Meg. I hope she's not a fussy eater.

'That would be great. Thank you so much. I'll eat anything,' she says as if reading my mind.

'Good, because it's bangers and mash,' says Roz.

Roz is in charge of the food department here at Oak Tree Lodge. Self-appointed. I'm not sure when that happened. It just evolved. She started bringing in groceries on a daily basis, and it suited everyone. Why wouldn't it? Shopping's a drag. It involves constant inventory lists and stock-taking. And then the fetching and carrying and stacking and putting away. The truly weird thing is that Roz is not actually interested in consuming any of the food. She just wants to be in control of it. It's as if, left untamed, the gingernuts or bacon rashers will get the better of her. I guess a psychologist would explain it as just another symptom of her obsessive-compulsive disorder.

Anyway, it suits everyone. Under Covid-19, people are not allowed to go to supermarkets in groups or even in pairs. There must be a designated shopper, a bit like a designated driver for an alcohol-infused party held in the middle of nowhere. Here at Oak Tree Lodge, we're already up to speed on that one.

'And garden salad,' Roz adds, with a sniff. She must be feeling a bit peckish. She'll probably dive into a radish and a piece of cos. 'We'll cook outside. Such a lovely evening. And it's safer out there, you know, from the virus,' she says, looking at Meg.

'Hey, well, let me take care of the bangers,' says Julius, springing up.

I always let Julius do the al-fresco cooking. Some guys seem to pop testosterone as soon as there is talk of a barbecue. Right now, Julius is eighty-per-cent steroids and a twenty-per-cent dangerous mix of adrenalin and dopamine, which makes him pretty volatile. I hope Poppy phones back. That would be something.

I can hear Frank at the piano. He's got an old upright set up on the front wall of his bedroom. He's playing Jazz. He never plays anything else. It's usually "As Time Goes By", and this afternoon is no exception. I don't mind Jazz. It's some time since he played, at least two weeks, about the time that Chelsea was no longer here. Frank is quite good on the keys. He never calls himself a musician, but he's good enough to have had a few gigs in the Piano Bar along the road.

So it's a dinner party then. It's been a while. The disappearance of Chelsea put a dampener on things. I excuse myself and race up the stairs. I need to carry out a little reconnaissance. It's not exactly a powder room visit, but I want to make sure I'm looking okay if I'm going to make a play for Meg. I also need to hide some stuff in case she wants to come up and see my etchings. I check myself out in the mirror. Nothing out of place, although I probably need to trim my moustache in the next day or two. It's amazing how thick and lush it is. My hair is another story. I spray a little mousse around where the scalp is showing and plump up the crown area.

I realise I haven't got my best jeans on, the ones that give me a bit more bulk. These are somewhat tight and, if I'm honest, a little on the short side. The girl who took them up didn't have any idea, so now, when I cross my legs (which I try not to do: it's not very manly), they ride up and show my socks and sometimes my ankles. I put them on this morning because I wasn't expecting the outside world, let alone Meg, who is an angel, to come visit.

I can't change now. That would not be cool. Dressing for dinner like the Earl of Grantham would definitely invite comment. No, the jeans will have to stay. I could probably get away with a change of shoes. No-one would notice that, not even Julius, who fancies himself as a kind of Poirot, sniffing out vital clues and bringing in scoops. I've got some boots that give me another inch. That would put me at eye level with Julius. And some. Definitely a risk worth taking.

I slip into the back of my wardrobe and gather Chelsea's stuff into a neat pile. I haven't got time to hide it away. I grab my robe and throw it over the top. A gold stiletto is peeping out. I kick it further in. Now it's upside down, and the heel has formed a little tent. I peel back the gown, grab the shoe, place it underneath Chelsea's bra and panties, and then cover it all up. That will have to do for now. I need to get downstairs.

Frank must have decided enough *time has gone by* because he's come out of his room. It's Frank Time. You can set your watch by it. Time for pre-dinner drinks. He's always in his wheelchair in the evenings. He can walk okay. He just finds it more comfortable on wheels. His wheelchair has a drink pouch on the right arm. His bottle of Steinlager, which he's half-way through, is a perfect fit. And there is room on his footrest for a six-pack. Frank drinks his beer warm. He says refrigeration is overrated and that man was designed to consume things as they come, blood temperature. Frank talks a lot about blood. I guess that's okay if you're an old guy. He probably thinks about his heart a lot and counts the beats to make sure they're still pumping the red stuff where it's meant to go.

But the biggest upside for Frank is that Roz fusses over him. Even though she knows full well that he can get up and walk, she enjoys the whole charade. So Frank gets to sit like a lord and be waited on. He's dressed for dinner. That's a first. He's swapped his checked shirt for a floral arrangement with the sleeves rolled up. He's stationed himself in the corner in front of the television, which is switched to CNN.

Julius has fired up the barbecue. It's a serious unit with slatted foldouts to rest the food on. He has taken off his tee-shirt and seems to be turning each movement into a pose, as if he's on stage, competing in a body-building competition. There's a dish of sausages and onion rings on the trays, and Julius is oiling the grill. Meg has joined him in the garden.

This is not the ideal setting for getting the girl. I've read up quite extensively on chat-up lines. You're supposed to ask something open-ended like, did you just see what happened outside in the street? Or, are you responsible for this beautiful evening? Or, if you're in a bar, you can have a cocktail sent over. None of this is going to work here.

Roz is layering the leaves of a cos over something reddish underneath, tomatoes and shredded carrot, by the look. She has buttered a whole loaf of white bread and covered it in plastic film. What happened to the mash, I am thinking.

'Looks like you're in for a treat, some real down-home Kiwi food,' I call to Meg as I step into the garden.

'I can't believe I'm here. This morning I had no place to go and no plan. Just goes to show, doesn't it? Sometimes it's best to let it be.' Meg has the sun behind her, and she's golden. But she's feeling the heat and has a moist look about her. She pushes her hair back from her forehead and wipes her brow. And then she lowers herself onto the grass and leans back, balancing herself on her elbows, and offering her face to the sky. I imagine myself leaning down to her and kissing her. It's clearly what she wants.

'Can I do anything?' I ask Julius. I know he hates letting anyone share his barbecue gigs. It's like asking if he needs a hand to fuck the girl.

'Nah, all good, mate.' He's turning the sausages. They're over-pricked and spitting fat onto the grill. He can't leave them alone. No wonder Poppy can't deal with him. Girls are just like meat on the burner when you think about it. They should be left in peace. Give them space and time, and they'll turn out just right. They'll come to you, ripe as a peach. As a rule. I'm not sure about Meg. I'm thinking different rules might apply to her.

'I'll let you get on,' I say. Julius is so intent on the sausages that he's forgotten the onions, which are beginning to burn on the edge of the grill. I don't eat onions. I go back inside.

Meg follows me. A good sign. Her glass is empty. I pour the last of the champagne for her and grab a beer from the fridge. I remind myself to drink it slowly.

And now Julius is coming back in with the sausages and what is left of the onions, and Roz is telling everyone to sit up as she lays out the bread and salad. I take my usual spot at the head of the table, and Meg sits on my right.

'Hey, Leo, how good is this?' she says.

'Guests first,' says Roz, spooning salad onto Meg's plate. And then she obviously considers her duties done because she fills her wine glass, grabs her cigarettes and heads for the garden. Frank has no choice but to wheel himself up to the table and help himself.

'Here, let me,' says Meg, piling up his plate.

'Looking this way,' says Julius, and he snaps a photo of us as if we're all one happy family.

'Just don't put it on Facebook, okay,' I say, hoping Julius gets the message that we're not going to star in his next bullshit journalism assignment.

I'm wondering about my next move when Meg picks up a sausage between the thumb and forefinger of her right hand and places it in the palm of her left hand. It's a deft movement, as if she's done it before. And then, she sucks the oil off her fingers and places the sausage on a piece of bread, which she rolls up. Julius misses this; he is looking at his phone, admiring his photojournalism. And Frank is intent on the TV.

And then she turns to me, opens her mouth wide, and slowly and deliberately inserts the sausage into her mouth.

CHAPTER SEVEN

THURSDAY 26th MARCH, FIRST DAY OF LOCKDOWN

Last night could have gone better. After the sausage incident, I thought I was in with a chance. Even before the sausage, I knew Meg liked me. She'd told me. Not in so many words, but as good as. What girl puts on red knickers and then flashes them?

A girl who wants to get in bed with you, that's who.

Go hard, go early, our PM keeps saying with regard to the coronavirus. I'm right behind her. It's a good motto for most things. I have decided to apply it to my relationship with Meg. No point in wasting time. Seize the day and all that.

The odds are a bit stacked against me. It's hard to woo someone when everyone is watching your every move. I tried to get Meg alone, so I could invite her upstairs for an after-dinner coffee or night-cap. This proved impossible. There was an evening update on the coronavirus. Everyone was gathered around the TV set. And then Meg announced that she was bushed and left the room.

Just like that. *Bushed.* I found that word very seductive and wondered if she was trying to tell me something. Anyway, I decided to leave it. It must have been a big day for her.

I'm a bit late down this morning. It's day one of lockdown, a historic day. It took a while to get myself together. I decided to trim my moustache. I usually let my barber do it. It's a job for a specialist. I got the setting wrong on my electric trimmer, and I've ended up with more upper lip exposed than I'd like. Fortunately, I found a back-up bottle of my special shampoo, so my scalp feels calm. And I rooted around in the cupboard and found some volumising conditioner. I've got my other jeans on and a chambray shirt. I've gone for smart casual.

I hope Meg likes the look.

I always leave the contact lens till last. I can see fine, more clearly than most, just not small things. For example, I can't read the newspaper or a book without glasses. Or the fine print on a shampoo bottle. This is particularly annoying because sometimes when I'm in the shower, I don't know whether I'm using shampoo or conditioner.

I try to restrict my use of glasses to just when I need to see tiny stuff. I want to protect my long-range vision, but also, I don't think I look my best with specs on. They clutter up my face and hide my eyes, which are my best feature. They're not overly large, but they're a nice colour: baby blue, so I've been told.

So the contact lenses are a recent part of my gig. I say lenses, but, actually, I've only got one — for my right eye. I had to undergo a barrage of tests. The optometrist was very professional. I had to read letters from a chart, first with one eye and then the other. And then I had to sit in front of a machine and put my chin on a ledge and hold still and read more stuff. Finally, I had to go into another room and do it all over again on yet another apparatus and look into a lens without blinking while my pupils were filmed hundreds of times.

The eye specialist was very soothing. She had a tinkly voice that was a bit hypnotic but also quite authoritative, so I felt as though I was in capable hands. I liked her. And she was especially nice when she showed me how to put a contact lens in. She scooped the lens out of its dish and perched it on the end of her forefinger and put it into the palm of my hand, and guided my own forefinger so that I was able to get it into the exact right position before inserting it into my eye. I have to admit I found it difficult to concentrate on this manoeuvre. I found her very tactile, and we were sitting close together in a somewhat darkened room. It took a couple of goes, but in the end, I got the hang of it.

The downside is that now I see too much: dust, for example. There seems to be dust everywhere I look. I guess that's the way with old houses. They're not exactly hermetically sealed, and the wind whistles in, especially around the windows and floorboards. And with that comes dirt. Oak Tree Lodge is on the main road. There's not much in the way of grass in the front to absorb grime. It's all out there, swirling on the street and footpaths. Edith, my cleaner, seemed to keep on top of this. I must remember to give her a pay rise after this is all over.

Another downside of my improved vision is that when I look in the mirror, I see a different person. I suppose what I am looking at is real. It must be what other people see. But I now know that my eyes are not that great. They're okay, but they're a bit more grey than blue if I'm honest. Ice-blue is what I would like them to be. Ice-blue.

The colour of decision.

I also notice that my hair is quite grey on the sides. I'm not so worried about this because I know it's a plus. It's distinguished, right? I've noticed Meg looking at my hair. Most people do. Hair is important. It's a whole résumé of a person, a curriculum vitae of sorts. It reveals vital information: age, virility, social status, health, wealth, everything really.

I didn't sleep well last night. The thought of Meg downstairs didn't help. I kept thinking she should have been up here with me. Such a waste. I know she wants it. Maybe she'd prefer that everything was kept under wraps, as it were. You see movies about that, don't you? Girl wants boy but makes him sneak out in the middle of the night after they've had sex so her flatmates don't twig and post her relationship status all over Facebook.

And there seemed to be a lot of noise coming from downstairs, not noise exactly, more like voices, a single voice to be exact: Meg's. It was urgent and fast, and there were a lot of pauses as if she was talking to someone on the phone. I guess she's entitled to talk to people. I suppose it was early morning in London. Must be hard to manage your social life from the other side of the world.

And then there were sirens and the sound of a chopper. That's not unusual around here. Cities create chaos. People drink too much and do stupid things. I guess Covid-19 doesn't mean much if you've got nothing to live for. There are a lot of homeless people. They congregate in the park in summer and the arcade in winter.

I'm on my way downstairs, and I'm looking at the photo on the wall by the linen cupboard. It's a grand piece. Black-and-white, framed in oak with a sepia border. It's a shot of a handsome couple on their wedding day, standing in a garden in front of a playing fountain. They look happy.

I love looking at this photo. I tell everyone it's my parents. But, actually, the couple is not my parents. This is not the only lie I've told about them. They're not dead, as I told Meg. They're still alive. Sort of. They're in an old folk's home in Remuera, that posh suburb where money grows on trees. I used to visit them. I don't anymore. They don't know me. They don't know each other either. Not really. Dementia does that. They wake up every morning and look at the world and each other in amazement. Who is this person, they are thinking. And then they get to spend the rest of the day getting used to each other all over again. Imagine that: life, a never-ending courtship.

There were warning signs: losing keys, forgetting people's names, getting lost, and then tears and tantrums and denial. The truly amazing thing is that my parents went into decline at almost exactly the same time. Alzheimer's is not contagious, not like Covid-19.

But it was in my parents' case. Mum was the first to show symptoms. She put a chicken in the microwave and completely forgot about it.

It was a relief, really.

I always hated them. It's hard to love parents who scream at you and lock you in your room, and hit you all the time just because you don't measure up to their impossible expectations.

At least they left me some money.

I don't think they really understood what they were doing when I got them to sign that cheque made out to me.

The couple I'm looking at is nothing like my mum and dad. It's just a random photo I picked up at a second-hand shop in the arcade down the road. I had it framed. Sometimes make-believe is easier than reality.

I jog the rest of the steps down. I want to announce myself. To Meg, mainly: let her know I'm in the kitchen, waiting for her. Ready.

Roz is an early riser. She's brought in the morning paper and laid it out on the garden trestle. She's squirting it with insect repellent.

'Well, hello there.' Meg has walked in, fresh and fragrant, although I'm pretty sure she didn't take a shower. I would have picked up on that. She has dressed for the heat: denim shorts and a skimpy top, which shows off her midriff. She has tied her hair back into a high ponytail. This makes her look very young. I notice she is wearing lip gloss. Meg uses her mouth a lot even when she's not speaking. It's her best feature. I think she knows this and plays to it.

'Hey, good morning to you. How did you sleep?' I say.

'I slept like a logarithm. I had a visitor in the night,' she says.

'Jesus, that Frank...' I say.

But Meg interrupts me with a laugh. 'I didn't know you had a cat. Well, I did know, but I didn't realise she was so friendly. Made herself right at home. Wouldn't take no for an answer.'

'Prince. His name is Prince. It's a boy cat. You should have put him out.'

'Oh, a boy cat, I should have known. I didn't have the heart. He seemed to be so happy, started purring the minute I let him in. And I didn't sneeze once. I normally come out in a rash.'

'That's Chelsea's cat.' This is from Roz. She's brought the paper in and has parked herself at the dining table. 'I feel sorry for him. He loved Chelsea, followed her around like a little dog. Strange, because cats aren't a bit like that, not normally. So now he doesn't know where he is. What's your star sign?' She's directed this question to Meg.

Roz is really quite socially challenged, I'm thinking. No *good morning, how did you sleep, must be hard in new digs, were you too hot?* Nothing. Normally, I wouldn't mind, but I don't want Meg judging me by the company I keep.

'It's Aries. You know, the ram,' says Meg. 'What am I in for today?' she asks. Friendly. I love her for that. So many girls are stuck up without having any business to be.

Roz runs her finger up to the top of the page and clears her throat. '*Even though you are not a newcomer to a situation, going in with a beginner's mind will increase your luck exponentially. Innocent and unbiased reception allows you to see and hear more.*'

'Hey, that's me. I love how those guys always get it right,' says Meg, looking at me.

'So that means your birthday is right around now,' says Roz, as if she's just solved the riddle of the Sphynx.

'Actually, it's Saturday.'

'That's the day after tomorrow!' squeals Roz.

'I guess it is,' says Meg. 'It'll be kinda quiet, but there's no place I'd rather be.'

'You must let me make you a cake, at least,' says Roz.

'Wow, that would be great,' says Meg. And it looks like she means it. She seems open to invitations.

In the mood. This is my chance to get her to myself. I just need to take the plunge.

'Hey, let me cook you something,' I say. 'Something special since there's no chance of a restaurant. You know, everything's shut.'

'Wow,' says Meg and she puts her right foot on her left leg, a charming pose, almost balletic. She really is very lithe, I'm noticing. 'I've got to stop saying wow all the time, but I honestly don't know what to say.' She's pouting a bit and undoing her hair, and then doing it up again as she says this.

'Yes would work,' I say.

'Yes, then,' says Meg.

And Roz has raised her thinly plucked eyebrows almost to her hairline. I know what she is thinking.

CHAPTER EIGHT

THURSDAY CONTINUED

The toilet is blocked.

Frank has done his business in there and then left a note on the whiteboard and gone out.

He's written "TOILET BLOCKED" and drawn an emoji of a sad face in the bottom right-hand corner below the cat's whiskers. It's where he leaves all his messages as if he's hoping that they will get missed. Does he think this is somehow funny? Because it's not even close to funny.

So here we are on the first day of lockdown, and I have to call a stranger to come into our bubble and fix the most germ-laden part of anyone's house. And, in the meantime, I'll have to share my bathroom with everyone.

Of course, Meg can come up any time. But Julius and Roz? And Frank?

'When did that happen?' I ask Roz, pointing at the whiteboard.

'It was all right earlier,' she says. 'No idea.'

'I'll need to call a plumber.'

'You can't do that,' says Roz sharply. 'We can't have a total stranger coming in here. There were seventy-eight new cases today. It's exponential. People are dying. Have you any idea what's going on out there? We can't take the risk. We won't know where any random plumber has been. Oh, God!' Roz has picked up the sanitiser and is pumping it and wringing her hands. 'No alternative unless you want to use the toilets in the arcade,' I say.

Roz looks at me as if I'm Hannibal Lecter. 'What's wrong with using your bathroom?' she asks, her voice rising.

Julius has walked in from the garden. His phone is ringing, and he's ignoring it. And then the ringing stops and starts again immediately with a different tone, way more strident.

'What's up?' I ask. Julius is looking a bit crumpled. He has put his tee-shirt back on, but it looks as though he's slept in it. And he's forgotten to put anything on his feet.

'I had a missed call. From Poppy,' he says, rubbing his scalp. 'I should ring her back.'

'So why don't you?' says Roz.

I'm glad for the diversion. I need time to think. I have to be decisive and a problem-solver while keeping Roz calm. I have to sort the blocked toilet for Meg. She's not saying anything, but I sense she's watching everything very closely.

'I plan to, but I don't want to phone her back if, you know, it's a bad time. I don't want to catch her when she's in the middle of something or whatever.'

'So maybe stay off your phone, in case she rings you,' suggests Roz. 'No wonder you keep missing calls.'

'I need to change my ringtone, make it more noise-proof. There's so much going on around here; I think it needs to be on outdoor mode.'

Julius is such a baby, I'm thinking. He really should stop sucking his thumb and get off the pot.

'A blocked toilet will lead to other things. If things get banked up, the next thing you know, we won't be able to take a shower or do the laundry,' I say. 'I have to call Noah. There really is no other way.'

Roz has grabbed the hand sanitiser again. 'Fine,' she says. 'Fine, fine,' she repeats in that way that means nothing is fine, and the world, as we know it, is about to end.

Noah, my plumber, picks up immediately. He's a no-nonsense type of guy. He loves drains and taps and water closets. He's also a cyclist, a fitness fanatic. He likes to go the distance with the wind in his hair. That figures. If you've been clearing blocked drains under old houses, close-up and personal with lagging and pipework, and, not to be indelicate, other people's shit, you might want to get out in the fresh air and look at the sky.

'Are you working at the moment?' I ask. 'You know, are you in the essential service category?'

'Depends,' he says. 'If you're installing a new vanity or dishwasher or just upgrading, then it's supposed to be a no. But I can't sit around all day with my thumb up my bum. What is it?'

'Well, it is kinda essential,' I say. 'The toilet's blocked.'

'Your lucky day,' he says. 'I'll be right over.' And he sounds as though he's just won lotto. I guess, in lockdown, business must be slow.

'Noah is on his way,' I say without looking at Roz.

'Oh, God,' says Roz. 'Oh, God,' she repeats. This is her mantra now. 'We all must keep our distance. We don't know where Noah's been, how many houses he's been in. And now he's coming into ours. He's breaking our bubble.'

'It's okay, Roz, I'll take care of it,' I say.

'I hope you get it,' says Roz. 'It's no good being all brave and thinking it's manly to take risks. You're putting everyone's life in danger when you do that. It's not your decision to make.'

And then there is a knocking at the door. Roz startles and jumps up, grabbing the sanitiser. 'I'm staying in my room until he goes,' she says, handing me the bottle. 'Make sure he uses this before he comes in,' she says. 'This is not just about me. We're all in this together. All of us need to keep away from him. Oh, God,' she says again and runs up the hallway into her bedroom.

'Maybe just stay in the garden,' I say to Meg. 'I have no idea how long this will take.'

'I'm fine,' says Meg. 'I was about to do some yoga, anyway. I'll just make myself some tea, and then I'll be floating. If I need to, can I use your, you know?'

'Sure,' I say, hoping Julius is not listening. I'm wondering if I should have phoned Noah in the first place. Was this my chance of getting Meg upstairs? I'm also wondering about Meg in her bedroom doing yoga. I'm picturing her doing downdogs or whatever. I've always found those body-bending poses very arousing. Girls get themselves into impossible positions which scream *take me now!* I watch it on TV sometimes. It's all about display, it seems to me. Whoever made up those poses was definitely male.

More knocking, and then the doorbell rings. I gulp down a glass of water and make for the front of the house.

I open the door to Noah. He's dressed for dirt: black denim, black tee, even his trainers are black. He's a small guy, wiry and lean, perfect for reaching into pipes and folding himself into corners. Sometimes you have to wonder about how much one's body type dictates one's station in life.

'Sorry, mate, house rules,' I say, as I hand him the sanitiser. Noah obliges, but he allows himself a smile.

'What's so funny?' I ask.

'How clean is your bog?' he asks.

'Just keeping the peace, mate,' I say. 'Covid-19 is making everyone crazy.'

'It's crazy out there on the street,' says Noah. 'People everywhere. We're supposed to be staying home. It's like the Mardi Gras.'

'What's going on?' asks Julius. He's followed me to the door.

'Something in the arcade. Police cars everywhere. The place is cordoned off. And there's not much social distancing going on. I can tell you that for nothing.'

'Did you see what it was?' asks Julius.

'There were a couple of ambulances; that's all I know.'

Julius is lit up like a Christmas tree. He disappears into his room.

'It's along here, right,' says Noah, making his way up the hall. 'Any babies here?' he asks.

'What?'

'Baby wipes: you have no idea how many toilets are full of them. They get jammed up and, before you know it, you've got slush city.'

I decide to ignore the question. Noah goes in and flushes the toilet. I go in with him and try to socially distance myself, not easy in a room designed for one.

'Okay, it's blocked,' he announces, unnecessarily, in my view. 'I need to go to the truck.' Noah has his truck parked in the driveway. He's back in a minute with what looks like a crank. I decide to leave him to it. What I really want to do is knock on Meg's door and ask her if she's doing okay. She might be in the middle of her warm-ups. I need to think of a reason. Maybe I could take her some fruit. I'm pretty sure she hasn't had breakfast. But I don't want to come across as pushy. That would be a turn-off. She's already agreed to have dinner with me. Maybe I just need to chill.

'I'm going to check out what's going on,' says Julius. He's come out of his room. He's wearing a cap and shades, and he's carrying a notebook. Christ, he's an ambulance chaser now. What a prick of a job. It suits him. And then he's gone.

'It's a no-go,' says Noah, coming out of the toilet. 'I'll need to try something else. Where's the sewer line?'

'Out back,' I say.

Noah follows me out and goes up the side of the house, where all the drains are. He crouches down and pulls a grill back from one of the outlets. I stand back and let him do his thing.

'The blockage could be anywhere.'

'So what's the plan?' I ask.

'What's in there?' Noah is indicating the shed.

'Nothing, it's just storage,' I say.

'Any pipework?' he asks. 'I might need to get in there. I don't want to be digging up your garden.' Noah says this with an expression on his face that tells me he can't wait to dig up the garden.

'There's an old tub,' I say. 'I never go in there. Honestly, I can't remember when I last even opened the door. It's locked, and I've lost track of the key.'

'Okay, let's try a probe. I've got some cable in the truck.' Noah is enjoying himself. A blocked toilet brings people to their knees. Noah knows this. The announcement of level four lockdown made toilet tissue top of people's shopping list. Panic buying emptied supermarkets. People loaded up their trolleys and fought in the aisles. The PM had to beg people *to be kind*. I think this was when the whole kindness idea began: over loo paper. Can you imagine that?

'Give me a minute,' he says and walks up the side of the house to his truck.

I'm wondering what all the fuss is about at the arcade. I remember hearing sirens in the night. I love Oak Tree Lodge, but sometimes I wish it was somewhere else, somewhere a bit more salubrious. There's a shoe repair shop to the left and a nail bar (I've only ever seen men with big hair and impossible heels in this establishment) to the right. Across the road is a massage parlour, invisible by day, neon-lit by night. And a bit further down, there are strip joints with explicit shop fronts. And, of course, there's the arcade. Who knows what goes on behind some of the locked doors? Cosmopolitan is what it is, a melting pot of people from all walks of life. It's an okay concept, but the reality can be a bit confronting at times, especially late at night.

'Where can I plug this in?' Noah is carrying a roll of cable and what looks like an electric motor. He hands me the lead to the motor. 'I'll feed this down and see what's what,' he says, indicating the cable, which has a hooking device at the end.

I push the lead through the kitchen window. 'How far will the cable reach?' I ask.

'There's plenty, just depends on how much shit is in there.' Noah seems to find this hilarious.

I go into the kitchen and plug in the lead. I really want to get this over with. I look out through the window. Noah is squatting by the drain, deep in thought. What can there possibly be to ponder?

Finally, the motor springs into life, and Noah feeds the cable down the drain.

'What's going on?' asks Roz. She's standing in the doorway of the kitchen.

'It's okay; Noah is outside. He's putting a probe down,' I say. And then the motor stops, and Noah is winding the cable back onto its roll. Roz joins me at the kitchen window, and we watch together as Noah draws a tiny, sludge-soaked garment from the drain.

'There's your culprit,' says Noah through the open window. 'Someone's knickers. Very sexy,' he adds, with a grin.

Of course, I recognise them immediately. The panties I found in the bathroom and flushed down the toilet. They belong to Roz. I expect her to apologise.

'I'm pretty sure Chelsea had a pair like that,' she says with distaste.

Roz is obviously mortified to have her underwear on display like this. And so she should be. They're not in the least bit sexy.

Unlike Chelsea's.

CHAPTER NINE

FRIDAY 27th MARCH

Someone died yesterday. And it wasn't anything to do with Covid-19.

It was a homicide. Julius came back from his reconnaissance with an empty notebook and little to report. So much for bearing witness and getting the story. The arcade was cordoned off and crawling with police, he said. No-one could get near. He talked to a few bystanders, who gave conflicting stories. The only thing that everyone seemed to agree on was that a young woman was found dead in the arcade. One person said that he was pretty sure she was one of the workers from Lollipops.

Today it is front page news. Roz has brought the newspaper in from the letterbox and is about to sanitise it when Julius snatches it up.

Roz snatches it back. 'You're a murderer!' she screams and takes it out into the garden. She's wearing gloves.

This is how things are here. If Roz had her way, we'd all be in hazmat suits. Julius switches the television to the news channel and watches while he waits. I'm not sure why he is so fascinated by the death of a young girl. It's hardly a one-off. Maybe he thinks he can uncover some fragment of information that will make him famous. He fancies himself as a newshound.

Poppy might forgive him if he starts writing about something other than her.

I'm more interested in what's happening tomorrow night. It's Meg's birthday dinner. She says she'll eat anything, but I want to play the chef. I'm thinking of starting with champagne to get her in the mood and then following up with seafood and a salad. I'll have to make a special trip to the supermarket. This is Roz's job normally. But her idea of romantic food won't cut it. This will be a mission. Roz will want to unpack what I bring into the house and give it a soapy shower. This won't work. Don't get me wrong. I'm all for safety and sanitising. I'm all in. Totally. But sometimes risks are worth taking.

Eventually, Roz disappears up the side of the house, abandoning her post by the paper. Julius gathers it up and brings it inside. He lays it out on the dining table.

'Listen up,' he says.

'You fixed it then. The toilet?' Frank has walked in, carrying a basket of laundry. He's wearing his usual hunting get-up. I'm wondering where he's been and whether he cleaned his hands when he came back. I'm glad Roz is not here.

'It's Friday,' I say.

Monday is washday for Frank. He knows this. There is a roster. Roz drew it up. She said there was only so much room on a washing line.

'Friday is a free day,' he says.

He's right. When Roz drew up her rota, she left Friday and Saturday free. For emergencies, she said. I'm wondering what Frank's emergency could possibly be.

'So the girl has been identified already,' says Julius. 'Janet Lane, although she went by the name of

Lily, Lily Lane. I guess that's a perfect name for a stripper. Lily Lane from Lollipops.'

I think I don't really need to hear Julius's ruminations.

'So what else does it say?' I ask. 'Does it actually say that's where she worked?'

'No, actually, but it wouldn't, would it? Newspapers have to be careful. They don't want to be accused of libel. They might get sued.'

'You can't sue a newspaper for reporting facts, however unpleasant,' I say. How can Julius not know this? I would have thought that would be in every primer for a journalism course.

'She was found early in the morning by a man out walking his dog,' Julius says, ignoring me.

'How early?' I ask.

'It doesn't say,' replies Julius. 'Actually, there's not much here, just that the police are treating it as a homicide and are calling for anyone to come forward if they have any information.'

'I guess there were no witnesses. There never are. You'd have to be pretty stupid not to have a look around before you decide to do away with someone,' I say.

'There's always CCTV,' says Julius. 'It'll all be recorded. You mark my words. It's just a matter of time.'

'Actually, Julius, I think you'll find there are absolutely no cameras in the arcade. There used to be. And then, the locals got together and signed a petition against them. They said they didn't want their comings and goings recorded for the whole world to see. And the businesses gave in. The likes of Lollipops was boycotted, and so they had no choice really.'

'Somebody must know something,' says Frank. 'She must have been doing something on the sly at Lollipops last night since it was supposed to be closed. And then what? She must have been followed when she left.'

'How do you know that?' asks Julius. He has a gotcha look about him as if Frank is on the stand in a courtroom, and he's the prosecuting attorney who's hit pay dirt.

'Well, I don't, but it's a no-brainer. Doesn't take a genius to work it out. A girl doesn't rape herself.'

'How do you know she was raped?' asks Julius.

'You just said so,' says Frank. 'And even if you didn't, it's obvious, isn't it? Who kills a girl without raping her first? What would be the point?' Frank looks down at his washing and takes it outside to the laundry.

Sometimes you have to wonder about Frank.

'Well, hello, Leo.' An angel has walked into the kitchen, and she's doing that "o" thing with her mouth again. Meg is wearing something very tight, dark against her pale skin. Is this her yoga get-up, I'm wondering. I haven't seen her since Noah came to fix the toilet.

'Hi, there,' I say. 'Where did you get to?'

'You know what,' says Meg, 'I just crashed. I did some yoga and then was out like a light. And then I woke up and watched a movie. Don't ask me what. Actually, it was sci-fi, sort of appropriate. I feel as though we're all in some parallel universe.' She's looking at me and wanting me to laugh, so I oblige.

'Wow,' I say. I want her to feel clever.

'I see the toilet's been fixed. You know how to get stuff done.' Meg goes to the sink and bends over to adjust the ties on her shoes. She is back-on to me so that

I get a clear view of her haunches. She is taut and even more slender than I noticed in the shower. She takes her time, and then she straightens up and does a little jig. This is all for my benefit. I'm thinking I can't wait until tomorrow night to see her with her clothes off.

'You hungry?' I ask.

'I'm always hungry,' she says, 'but I'm sort of on a diet. Besides, I'm saving up for tomorrow night. Oh, and I need to know, what can I bring?' She's right next to me now, and I am picking up her scent. It's floral. But also a bit musky. Meg doesn't strike me as the sort to wear perfume. There's something no-nonsense about her. This is natural, her essence, the smell of her skin, and I'm wanting to touch her.

'Just bring yourself. I could, you know, come pick you up if you like. In case you can't find your way.'

'Chivalry will get you everywhere,' says Meg, laughing. She has a beautiful laugh. It's not high-pitched and giggly. It has a deep resonance to it, almost a reluctance as if it's a precious gift bestowed only on rare occasions on the truly witty. It makes me feel good.

'But, seriously, I'll go get some wine. At least let me do that,' she says. 'Red or white?'

'You choose,' I say.

'Okay. Hey, I'm going for a walk. We're allowed to do that, right, as long as we stay close? To home, that is. And socially distance, right?'

'Sure, do you want me to come with you?' I know as soon as I say this, it is wrong. What girl wants a virtual stranger to accompany her for a walk? It's tantamount to stalking. And it doesn't make my joke about picking her up for our dinner date look so hot.

'I think I'll be okay, Leo,' says Meg. She's smiling at me, but her eyes aren't joining in. I really have to smarten up and bring my A-game to this courtship.

'I'll come with you,' says Julius. 'I need to get a closer look around Lollipops. And the wine shop is on the way. I'll show you where it is. Let me get my notebook.'

'Oh, okay,' says Meg, 'if it's not out of your way. I'll just get my phone.' She's doing that jigging thing again and moving her head a lot. She's got her hair tied back quite tight in a high ponytail. It's not my favourite hair style, but Meg pulls it off. I guess that's her yoga thing. Her messy look is tamed into a long tress. It bounces as she moves her head, and I want to grab it and pull her to me.

Keep calm, Leo. Breathe. It's just a walk. Meg would prefer to be on her own. She's made that crystal clear to all except that self-absorbed jerk, Julius, who really is autistic, I'm beginning to realise. Julius ambushed her. Meg couldn't really say no. That would have appeared rude. I must admit it was a clever move on his part to say, I'm going that way, anyway. There's no escape from this. It's like the guy who lives in Florida and shows up outside the girl's apartment in New York one snowy night in winter and says he happened to be in the area. He's obviously lying, but there's a cogency to it that is inescapable.

Frank has managed to get his washing on the line. But, in doing so, he's somehow bumped his hairpiece. I try not to notice or think about Frank's hair. I certainly never make any comment. I feel for him. It must be galling to have lost so much hair that you have to go out and purchase a whole replacement lot and glue it on. Right now, I'm thinking he didn't apply enough adherent because it's slipped to the left and everything about him looks sad and old.

'Where did you get to Wednesday night?' says Roz. She's come in through the back door and is clutching a bunch of parsley. Roz has a huge herb garden. It's at the back of the lot next to her compost. She says herbs ward off evil spirits. She's also got a yucca in a terra cotta pot. It's a miserable-looking thing with pointy foliage, a bit like Roz.

'What do you mean?' says Frank. I can't bring myself to look at either of them. Sometimes I wonder if I'm cut out to be a landlord. People are hell on wheels. There's no other way to put it.

'You went out. It was very late.'

I know Roz couldn't care less where Frank goes late at night or any other time. The coronavirus has changed everything. Paranoia is everywhere.

'I didn't go anywhere,' says Frank. 'Except to my room. And, anyway, what business is it of yours? I pay rent here the same as anyone else. Right, Leo?'

'Too right,' I say. The last thing I want is an argument. I know Meg has nowhere else to go, but I want her to be relaxed here at Oak Tree Lodge. I pride myself on running a happy ship with a cool vibe.

'Here, Frank,' I say, 'let me get this,' and I take the washing basket from him so that he can go back to his room and check out his hair. I know he's got a mirror in there, one of those full-length jobs.

CHAPTER TEN

SATURDAY 28th MARCH

I haven't been able to get seafood. And my hair is a mess.

I try to avoid taking diazepam, but tonight is going to be an exception. I'm hyper-alert about Meg's birthday and had a panic attack as soon as I got out of bed. I've tried to take deep breaths, but it's not working. I dig out my pill bottle, which I've got stowed at the back of my bathroom cabinet. I've only one capsule left. I'd like to take one now, but maybe I'll save it for later.

Roz hasn't forgotten her cake promise. She's already done a run to the shops and brought back the ingredients. She's put them outside in the garden and is making trips in and out to retrieve what she needs. She's wearing an apron, and the oven is switched to fan-bake.

'Chocolate or banana?' I ask her. She's carrying two eggs in her gloved hands and is headed for the sink of soapy water. I can't think of anything safer from the virus than a freshly opened egg, but I don't say anything.

'It's a surprise,' says Roz without looking at me. 'How old is Meg?' she asks.

'How should I know?' I say. 'Just one candle will be perfect.'

Julius is bent over the newspaper. He's poring over the front page, which seems to be all about the latest coronavirus cases.

'How's your assignment going?' I ask. 'Is there a deadline?' What I really want to ask is how his walk with Meg went yesterday.

'I'm taking it slow,' says Julius. 'I'll know more after the police have been.'

'What do you mean?' I ask.

'They're going door-to-door. Routine enquiries. We'll be on the list.'

'How do you know that?' I ask.

'They map it out. The scene of the crime is the epicentre, and they make a grid, starting with a radius of a kilometre and moving out from there. Oak Tree is very close as the crow flies. So they'll be here, if not today, then sometime tomorrow.' Julius takes a pen from his shirt pocket and scribbles something on the front of the newspaper.

I'm thinking Julius has been watching too much *Crime and Investigation* on TV. It's on the tip of my tongue to ask about Poppy. I decide to leave that for later. Right now, I've got more important things to concentrate on, like the menu for tonight's birthday dinner with Meg. I've opted for vegetarian pasta. There's a convenience store just around the corner. It sells bread and milk and canned food. There's a bargain box at the front with stuff past its use-by-date. Some of it looks pre-war. I give it a miss and walk the extra distance to the supermarket. Shoppers are queuing outside, a metre apart. There are lines on the pavement. Officials in red hats and white shirts are in attendance. There is a stand set up by the door with a sanitiser, and people are using their elbows to depress the stopper.

I get in and out as fast as I can. The aisles are all marked up with arrows painted on the floors to create a one-way system. If you weren't worried about Covid-19 before you left home this morning, a trip to this supermarket is guaranteed to change all that. I feel as though I'm on borrowed time. It's worse than that. I feel as though I've signed my death warrant. I'm going home, and I won't be coming back here any time soon. Roz can do the shopping from now on. Designated shoppers, there's a lot to be said for them.

I manage to let myself in and get my groceries upstairs unseen. I'm pleased with my dinner choice. It ticks all the boxes: lots of vegetables without looking vegetarian, tasty and creamy without being heavy, and, best of all, it's quite spectacular. A dish for a dish.

It's a Jamie Oliver staple. I've watched him make this on TV. He talks the whole time he is prepping his dishes. I admire him for that. He says disarming and counterintuitive things like, this is so simple to make that I feel my head is ready for lift-off. He gets your attention. Actually, it's not at all simple. In fact, it's quite fiddly. But it has the decided advantage of being a one-pot wonder. My dining table is strictly a two-setting affair, and I need room for candles and napkins and wine glasses.

Ordinarily, obviously, I would take a girlfriend prospect out to dinner. You know, wine and dine her, spoil her, make her feel like a princess. But these are extraordinary times. Restaurants and bars and clubs are closed. Such a pity. I know how to do things right, how to treat a girl. I'm especially suave in restaurants. I know how to greet the maître d', speak his language, read a menu, choose the right wine and make scintillating conversation.

But I have to be thankful. Every cloud and all that. If it weren't for lockdown, Meg wouldn't be here. I would never have met her. I find myself blessing lockdown. Blessing the virus. It's handed me Meg. On a platter. She's here for the duration. A captive, my captive.

Covid and Cupid. The words are practically the same. A difference of only two letters. Funny, isn't it? A deadly virus, carried on the wind, microscopic and mighty, powerful and unstoppable. And inscrutable. A mystery. Exactly like true love — which is what Meg and I have.

I haven't seen her at all today. But then I haven't gone looking for her. And she's stayed out of sight. It's that day-before thing, a bit like a bride and groom before their wedding. This is how I'm feeling, and Meg obviously feels the same.

To be honest, I've been busy all day getting everything ready. I'm big on linen. I've got a whole cupboard full of it in my bathroom, but only one set that's unused. It's at the back where I keep stuff that's special. I reach in and pull it out. I slide the wrapping off (it's in tissue) and open it out. I've been saving this for the right occasion. Meg is the right occasion. Do I need to iron it, I'm wondering. The folds are deep and ingrained. I don't really have time. There's too much else to do. I make up the bed and smooth the sheets out as much as I can. They're crisp and very white, with a high thread count. Egyptian cotton. They're soft but also firm, a no-nonsense, luxurious fabric. It sums me up when I think about it. No-nonsense and firm. That's definitely me. I know Meg will appreciate this. She's a class act.

I've also laid out fresh towels and cleaned the bathroom. I really need to stay on top of this. I notice there are a few spots of mildew in the shower cubicle. I have to persuade Edith to come back. She shouldn't be so afraid. We're a bubble here at Oak Tree Lodge. Roz makes sure of this.

I wasn't sure what to do about wine. Meg says she is bringing some, but I can't presume. It happens all the time, doesn't it? People promise to turn up with a salad at a pot-luck dinner and arrive with a block of cheddar because it's easier, or they just plain forgot. So I bought a bottle of champagne. I can't go wrong with that. What girl can resist a flute of bubbles? Certainly not Meg. She's already proved that.

I'm less certain about the music. I want to play Sibelius. But is that too individualistic? Should I be opting for something more eclectic, a playlist? Maybe I'll start with the classical and see how it goes down. Music is such a mood enhancer. I can't afford to get it wrong.

I've laid the table and have everything under control, well ahead of time.

Or so I thought. The truly big challenge turns out to be my hair. It's very hot today and even hotter upstairs in my apartment, so I've ended up sweating a lot. And that is never good for hair, especially if it's as fine as mine. I've got a high-strand count, a bit like Egyptian cotton, easily creased and high-maintenance, especially around the crown.

To cut a long story short, I have to start all over again with less than an hour to go. I decide to skip the Nizoral (it's full of chemicals, and I don't want to smell like a pharmacy) and go for the collagen and chamomile-enriched gel that I purchased before lockdown. This works really well, but the solution does seem to cling a bit, and it takes a lot longer than usual to dry my hair.

I'm in the middle of all this when I hear Roz's voice.

'Yoo, hoo,' she is calling. Roz has never been up here before, and I am reluctant to let her in. I'm wondering if I can ignore her, but she must have heard the hairdryer.

'Yoo, hoo,' she calls again.

'Hi, Roz,' I say, opening the door a fraction.

'I've finished the cake.' And she pushes her way into the room and lays it on the dining table. 'What a lovely flat,' she says, scanning the room. And now she is looking towards the bedroom. 'Are you going to show me around?' she asks.

'Another time, Roz. I've got a lot to get through,' I say.

'Suit yourself,' says Roz. 'Don't forget to put your boots on.'

CHAPTER ELEVEN

I'm sliding on my boots when there is a rap on the door. I haven't taken the diazepam, and I should have because there is a thundering in my chest.

'Just a minute,' I call out.

Meg obviously hasn't heard me because, all at once, she has walked in.

'Well, look at you, Leo,' she coos.

And, at that moment, right then and there, I know Meg is up for it. She's wearing a sleeveless shirt tied at the waist and a micro-skirt with a thigh-split. She's tilted her head up so that her mouth is the most prominent part of her face. That lip-gel again. Lolita in lip gloss. Was there such a thing way back then? Meg's holding two bottles of wine, which she holds out to me.

I take them from her without checking the labels. I've always thought it gauche to appraise a gift of wine. Everyone recognises an expensive label when they see one, don't they? That's why I've bought the real thing, something actually produced in France. I take her wine into the kitchen and grab the champagne. I realise I haven't said anything yet. Sometimes silence is the most eloquent communication of all. I pop the cork and take it to the table. I pour two glasses.

Meg has gone to the window and is looking out over the garden. It's late afternoon, and the sun is streaming in and gilding her hair. She's wearing it loose. It's very sexy. I walk over to the window and hold out the champagne.

'Happy birthday,' I say.

Meg pouts her lips over the rim of her glass and takes a sip.

And now, somehow, the cat, Prince, is in the room. He is rubbing himself up against Meg. She bends down to pick him up, and he immediately scampers away towards the bedroom. I follow him, and he runs into the wardrobe. I have forgotten to put Chelsea's things away. Prince has made a beeline for her bra and panties (he must be able to smell them under my robe) and is stretching himself out on top of them. I slide my clothes across into a more concealing position and close the wardrobe door.

I take the opportunity to pop the diazepam and then go back to Meg.

'You're the rooster in the roost. It's kind of trippy,' says Meg.

'Nice trippy, I hope,' I say. I like the rooster metaphor. It's very erotic and suggestive. Meg is sending me a signal. 'Shall we sit down? I'll put some music on,' I say. I've got a single chair and a three-seater. I'm hoping Meg takes the three-seater. It will be another signal. I flip on Sibelius: *Finlandia*.

'You have such good taste,' says Meg, arranging herself on the couch. She crosses her legs, and her skirt rides up. Any higher and her underwear would be on full display. She looks up at me. Her eyes are wide and serious.

I'm taking her skirt off, and she is kissing me. And I've got my hands under her top, and she is holding on to me and rubbing herself against me and whimpering. And then she is reaching down and unzipping my jeans and working them down and working me, and we are on the floor, and she is on top of me.

In my head. Only in my head. Stay in control, Leo, I tell myself. Take this slow. Girls like to flirt and flirt and then flirt some more. I have to make her want me. She has to be desperate, gagging for it, which I know she will be soon enough.

'Come on,' I say, 'I'll top you up.'

Meg leans back into the couch and uncrosses her legs, which she parts. I can't see what I want to see because I'm standing above her.

'Who's the cute couple in the photo on the stairs?' she asks, tilting her glass as I pour.

'Mum and Dad,' I say. 'On their wedding day.'

'They look so happy. And beautiful.' she says. 'Like their son,' she adds, gazing up at me.

'Not as beautiful as you,' I say.

'Flattery will get you everywhere,' she says, patting the seat of the couch. 'Are you going to stand there all day? Come, sit with me. I won't eat you.'

I'm hoping she will eat me, and I know that's her plan. A cool breeze floats in through the shutters. I'm glad of it. I'm way too hot. I sit next to Meg and twist myself towards her. I'm thinking this would be more comfortable if we were stretched out in the bedroom. I'm trying to assess the situation. Sex before dinner or after dinner? I'm not sure. It's a bit like that how-many-dates-before-sex question. Some girls are insulted if you so much as try to kiss them on a first date. I've read about this. And then you get the types who are devastated if you don't put the moves on straight away. It makes them feel undesirable. And ugly. And they never forgive you for it. I'm thinking I might put my arm around Meg and see how that goes down, when she suddenly stands up and goes to the window. 'Phew, I'm not used to this heat,' she says, fanning herself. 'What's in the shed?'

'Oh, you know, bits and bobs,' I say.

'Must be valuable,' she says, without turning around. Meg is doing that one-legged stand again, a ballerina pose, except that she's holding a glass of champagne. She really has fine legs, long and slender.

'It's mainly junk,' I say.

'You keep it locked up, though,' says Meg, turning to me.

'I've got all my tools in there,' I say. I'm not enjoying this conversation, which is about as unsexy as it gets. 'Hey, tell me about you. What's it like living in London?'

'It's crazy. Not so bad now that cars have to pay to drive into the centre. But very built up, nothing like Aotearoa.' She pronounces each vowel separately, and her tongue is doing a lot. I'm thinking this is the perfect word for Lolita's mouth. 'Did I get that right?' she asks.

Of course, Meg hasn't got it right, but I love her for trying. 'You're a natural,' I say.

She laughs that deep, joyous rumble of hers. It's the sexiest sound in the world. 'We live in a mews, which is a fancy word for a horse stable,' she says. She comes back to the couch and sits down. She's very close to me now, and I can't help wondering if she went to the window so she could showcase her legs. Show me what she's got, seduce me. As if she needed to do that. What a body. She really is a doll.

'Britain is very posh, isn't it?' I say.

'Not really. People get that idea because of the Queen. And Boris Johnson. He went to Oxford and talks posh. Most people can't even understand what he's saying. He thinks he's Winston Churchill.'

'Are you glad you're here?' I ask. Of course, by *here*, I mean upstairs in my flat, sitting next to me on the sofa.

'Put it this way,' says Meg, 'I don't miss London. I mean, I miss some things, being able to walk in St James' Park, and along the Thames, and shopping in Oxford Street, but I don't miss the madness, the crush. And the Tube: you know, sandwiched amongst strangers, with the person whose elbow is in your back and breath in your face, pretending you don't exist. All this, while you're hurtling along at speed, fifty metres underground.'

'Sounds like hell,' I say. Sounds like heaven, I'm thinking. To be that close to girls without having to ask permission or pass an eligibility test. Or even be seen.

'Here, there is all the space in the world. I wish I had been born here,' says Meg.

'So what do you do, you know, normally when you're not experiencing the great outdoors on the other side of the world?'

Meg takes a sip of her wine and then places her glass on the table by the couch. It's an occasional table. It's not one of those cheap cane box-like things with a glass top. It's oak, solid, with Queen Anne legs. It's a bit old-fashioned, but it matches the couch, which is high-backed with curved timber arms. All my furniture has come from antique shops. I wanted to create the right ambience, although, I must admit, right now, I'd give anything to be sprawled out on a deep-cushioned daybed with Meg snuggled in.

'I'm a nurse. I haven't actually done much nursing yet, but I've finished my studies and done my training. Now comes the hard part.' I like the way she says *hard part*. She's smirking as she says this as if she is thinking of yours truly. She shimmies up the sofa and crosses her legs, and then she uncrosses them and folds them under her. She's wearing black panties, and her skin looks very white against them. I think she's telling me to *come and get it*. What other message can there be? And then, she stretches and reaches over to pick up her glass. Her top shifts up, and, at this point, there is way more flesh on display than garment.

I can't help noticing that Meg isn't wearing any jewellery. I like girls au naturel. It's refreshing and girly. I've always thought there's a direct correlation between jewellery and age. Ropes of gold and pearls and diamond rings are adornments worn by desperate women trying to compensate for sagging jowls and age-spots. Meg doesn't even wear a ring. She has long, slender fingers. They look strong and supple: piano fingers. I bet they would feel good on my skin. I say she doesn't wear a ring, but it looks as though she might have at one time. Her ring finger has a little white circle around it where a band would usually sit, and the skin is a bit indented. Maybe she used to wear a ring to protect herself from unwanted attention. If so, she's taken it off. She must have removed it when she came here. That makes sense. She probably slipped it off as soon as she walked into the lobby and saw me.

'Are you looking forward to it?'

'Oh, sure, I like looking after people, making them feel better, helping them. Florence Nightingale, that's me. Not ICU stuff, though. I'm not into that. Or ER: way too gory. People come in with broken bones and knife wounds and lost fingers and all kinds of shit. Actually, I'm a bit allergic to blood. Haemophobic, like

Doc Martin. Crazy, I know. I should have been a teacher or something.' Meg has finished her glass of wine, and so have I. I realise I've been keeping up with her, and I'm feeling a bit buzzed.

'Here, let me get this,' I say, and I take her glass to the kitchen. I fetch two new glasses and open one of her bottles of wine. It's a New Zealand sauvignon blanc. I pour two decent wallops and bend down to check the oven.

'What's in there?' Meg has followed me into the kitchen. She's looking everywhere, appraising everything in that way of hers, as if she's a potential buyer about to submit an offer.

'Nearly there,' I say, handing her a glass of wine.

'I hope it's okay,' she says. 'I know nothing about New Zealand wine. I just asked the guy in the shop.' She lifts the glass to her mouth a little too quickly, and some of the wine ends up on her shirt. Meg tries to rub it off, but the fabric must be quite delicate, silk or something, because it has soaked up the liquid in a second and taken on that wet tee-shirt look. Meg looks down at herself and then up at me. She has beautiful eyelashes, long and lush and dark against her alabaster skin.

'Where is your bathroom?' she asks, heading to the door off the kitchen.

Finlandia is coming to an end, and I'm thinking of leaving it on a loop. If it ain't broke and all that. Meg is definitely in the mood. I need to keep the vibe going. I decide to light the candles. There's still a lot of late sun filtering in through the shutters, but it's not just about the light, is it? It's about atmosphere. Sibelius by candlelight. It doesn't get any better than this. It's just a matter of having the right girl, the classy girl, who appreciates stuff. I often think about that girl from Cranberry's. She really had no idea. She was pleasant enough, but there's no getting away from it; she was too plump and, actually, quite forward in a vulgar way. That's just not me. And that Chelsea girl was not much better. There is one big difference between the two. Miss Cranberry would have been *grateful*. She would have been accommodating and obliging and then said *thank you*. *Thank you very much*, is what she would have said. The same could not be said for Chelsea. She was fun and flirty, but when it came down to it, there was nothing doing. Those girls deserve what they get.

Meg is a long time in the bathroom. That's fine with me. Girls like to check themselves out—especially when sex is on the menu. There's a lot of prepping required. Fine. Take your time, Meg. Take all the time you need. I know you're in there making yourself ready for me.

There's a phone ringing downstairs. It's the same ringtone that I heard the other night. Meg has left her phone in her room when she came up to see me. She didn't want anything to get in the way of our evening. She really is perfection. There's no other way of describing her.

CHAPTER TWELVE

'Where were we?' says Meg. She has come out of the bathroom. She looks a bit different. Her face is pink, as if she has been running or something. Maybe she's just flushed with excitement. I wouldn't blame her. I notice her glass is almost empty. She walks back to the sofa and drops down onto it.

I've got a wine bucket at the ready. I filled it with ice and wedged the bottle in. I aim to keep Meg topped up, but I need to take it easy. I'm not at my best with too much alcohol on board. And I really don't want to let myself down. At the same time, I don't want to come across as uncool.

'Wow, you're my wine waiter and food waiter and escort, all rolled into one,' says Meg, as I lay the chiller on the table. She's doing that big smile again that involves her nose. When she laughs, it turns up a bit at the end and looks less patrician. I like this. Meg has lovely green eyes, soft and pale. They are steady and clear, even when she is laughing. I like this too. Eyes are important. I feel with Meg that she is really looking at me, you know, *seeing* me. And that's got to be a good thing, right? So many girls only see what they want to see.

She holds out her wine glass, and I fill it. 'Just a slash,' she says, doing that lisping thing with her tongue. 'Loving the candles,' she says breathily.

I'm thinking I need to move things along. Meg is more than ready, that's obvious, but I don't want to have sex with a drunk. Where's the win in that?

'Ready to eat, birthday girl?' I ask.

Meg nods. She's back in her yoga position with her legs folded under her so that she's a good deal taller than me as we sit on the couch. I'm finding this awkward.

'What can I do to help?' she asks, flicking her hair back. That Lolita mouth again. It's inches from me, and I can smell Meg's breath. It is sweet and minty, almost as if she has mouth-washed in the bathroom.

'Find yourself a seat at the table,' I say.

I have everything already set up, right down to serving spoons. I'm hoping Meg likes pasta. It's looking perfect, all hot and bubbly. Thank you, Jamie, I'm thinking. I especially like the melted mozzarella on top. It's soft and firm at the same time, the perfect consistency. Sexy. Exactly like Meg.

Meg is facing the window so that the dying rays of the sun are on her face and hair. She is almost too beautiful to look at. You hear about that, don't you, especially with music? She's the siren singer who drove the Odysseus crew mad with lust until they blocked up their ears with wax.

I take the seat opposite her and lift the lid off the casserole.

'Oh my God!' squeals Meg. She leans back in the chair and unties her top. She has a dark mole right in the centre of her midriff. It is beckoning to me, and I want to touch it.

'Don't make me fat,' she says as I ladle pasta onto her plate. 'I can't do fat.' She is stretching and showing off her tiny waist as she says this and sipping her wine at the same time, her Lolita lips caressing the rim of her glass.

I really need to get on with things while I still can. I manage to get some food onto my plate. I'm in the kitchen returning the casserole to the oven when I hear a cell-phone. It's the sound of an incoming message. I know it's not my phone. I've turned it off. And Meg's phone is downstairs.

Or so I thought.

When I come back in, Meg is looking at her device. She's texting. She doesn't see me seeing her. She looks different as if she doesn't like the message on her screen. And then, she stops texting and slips her phone into the back of her skirt. There must be a pocket in there somewhere. I haven't noticed.

I think about asking her who's texting her. But I've seen enough movies to know that this line of questioning can set a girl off. You know, *so I can't have my own life now, do you have to know my every movement?* This question is usually delivered at the high end of a screech and is guaranteed to be a precursor to sleeping in different bedrooms. This, I definitely don't want. So I elect to say nothing.

This is a good decision because Meg is behaving as if nothing has happened. She is holding her glass up high, ready for a toast. I take my seat and pick up my glass.

'Here's to Oak Tree Lodge,' she says.

'And all who reside there,' I say.

'Roger that,' she says and adds, 'no pun intended.'

I really love this girl; she's a total babe, and her pun is not lost on me. I know it is fully intended. I get you, Meg, I'm thinking. This is your birthday, and you are about to get the birthday present of your dreams. We just need to get this dinner over.

'Dig in,' I say, and I fork a load of pasta into my mouth.

Meg watches me and then follows my lead. But she's not just eating the pasta; she's making love to it and me at the same time. It's like a scene out of "Tom Jones" with Albert Finney and Joyce Redman, where they rape the food and then have raunchy sex in the bedroom.

Meg licks the spoon after each mouthful as if she's desperate for more.

And now I am opening up the second bottle of wine that Meg brought. It's pink, I think. I'm not really sure what it is, but I don't have to apologise for it. It was her choice, or maybe the wine guy's choice, but whatever, I'll go with the flow. I refill our glasses and slide them into the bucket

'What's that noise?' asks Meg. And with that, she is making for the bedroom. Perfect. That's where I want her. I didn't hear anything. This is her excuse to get me into bed. She's done with waiting. But now Prince has darted into the dining room. He has something balled up in his mouth. It looks like Chelsea's panties. Meg has followed him out and is reaching down and calling to him. I grab him and carry him back to the bedroom. I try to get him to open his mouth, but it's clamped shut. I fling him back in the wardrobe and close the door.

'Poor Prince,' says Meg. 'I guess he's missing Chelsea. But he loves you.' She's back on the couch, and I join her.

'Cats are like fallen leaves: they go wherever the wind blows them,' I say.

'What actually happened to Chelsea? I mean, what really happened?' asks Meg, and she leans into me and nudges my arm.

'Search me,' I say.

'Come on,' says Meg. She takes a sip of her wine and turns to me, eyebrows raised.

'It's anyone's guess,' I say.

'What's your guess?' says Meg. She picks up my glass of wine from the side-table and hands it to me.

'I really don't know,' I say. 'I felt sorry for her, actually, if I'm honest. She wanted to act, you know, in amateur dramatics, but she was a no-talent. The only acting I saw was what she put on in real life. She wasn't a very straight person.'

'People don't vanish just because they're disappointed,' says Meg. 'Do you think Quentin was involved, somehow?'

'It's usually the boyfriend. No, scratch that, it's *always* the boyfriend,' I say.

'Except that he seemed so frantic when he came. You know, genuinely distraught.'

'Yes, he did, didn't he?' I say. I am cursing myself for not putting Chelsea's stuff away. I really need to get Prince out of the wardrobe. Suddenly the bedroom is off-limits. This is really putting a dampener on things.

'You have a divine bed,' says Meg. She's jumped up and folded her legs under her again so that she's looking down on me a little.

'It suits the house,' I say.

'It suits you,' says Meg. 'It's big and classy.'

I can't think what to say to this. I'm feeling a bit light-headed. And now Meg is taking charge of the wine and refilling our glasses. Fine, why not? I'm not driving anywhere. I'm not even going anywhere. Except to bed, with Meg, when I can figure out what to do with Prince.

'I wish I could have met Chelsea,' says Meg. 'It's weird that I'm sleeping in her old room, in her bed. I feel as though I know her a little bit.'

'Really?' I say. I want to change the subject.

'It's the strangest thing,' says Meg, 'but sometimes I feel as though she is right there in the room with me. Old houses are a bit like that, aren't they? You know, they seem to absorb the essence of their occupants.'

I really need to get off the topic of Chelsea and all this spooky stuff. I'm thinking Meg has had too much to drink. And now she is getting up again and heading for the bathroom. I've noticed this with girls. Take Roz, for example; once she gets going on the wine, she's in the bathroom about every ten minutes. This is my chance to extract Prince. I race into the bedroom, fling open the wardrobe and fold back my clothes. I scan the floor. No sign of him. There's a hatch right at the back of the wardrobe that leads into the rafters. I always leave this open for ventilation. He must have gone walkabout in there with Chelsea's knickers. I slide the hatch cover back, move my clothes back and shut the wardrobe door. And then I flick the bedside light on. It's low wattage: sixty watts: seduction-sixty. That's what the girl in the light shop told me when she was giving me the eye.

And now Meg has come into the bedroom. She is carrying both glasses of wine. She hands me mine. She must have topped them up again because mine is quite full. She's looking at the painting of Venus with her head on one side in a pose of appraisal.

'Women in those days were gorgeous, weren't they?' she says. 'They weren't afraid of themselves.' Meg takes a deep breath and thrusts her breasts forward as if to demonstrate that she's not afraid of herself. *Here I am, come, get me,* she is saying. And then she turns away and walks towards the bed and the painting of the melting clocks. 'Hey, I've seen this before, I think.'

'It's just a print,' I say. This is possibly the most stupid thing I've ever said: as if anyone could have the original painting hanging in their bedroom. I'm pretty sure it's hanging in some gallery in New York.

'I've never been able to understand it,' says Meg. She moves closer to the bed and stretches herself out on it, crossing her ankles. Her skirt has folded itself up, and most of her thighs are showing. I'm trying to remember if I took the diazepam. I'm fairly certain I did. I'm hoping it will kick in soon.

'Explain it to me. I mean, I know it's supposed to be surreal or whatever, but what's the point of it?' says Meg. She's balancing her glass on her midriff, and there is moisture forming around her belly button.

I finish my wine in one gulp and place the glass on the floor next to the bed. Meg sits up suddenly and drains her glass. I take it from her and put it next to mine on the floor.

'People are obsessed with time,' I say. 'When you think about it, they're always checking their watches, wanting more time if they're trying to get somewhere, and less time if they're waiting for something to happen. Either way, they're trying to alter the progress of the ticking clock, never happy to let things be. *Just chill;* that's the theme of the painting. Writ large. You just have to look.'

Of course, I don't think Dali was saying anything of the sort. This is my message to Meg. I want her to forget about everything when I start to take her clothes off. I think she's hot for it right now. I'm getting a strong vibe that she is ready and waiting. More than ready: desperate. I also feel that I need to get on with things. I'm losing energy. In fact, I'm feeling a bit woozy, the way I get when I drink too much. I'm turning into Dali's melting clock. I lie down next to Meg and try to concentrate on my next move.

CHAPTER THIRTEEN

SUNDAY 29th MARCH

I'm awake, and somehow a meerkat has moved into my head. Along with the whole family. A mob. A mob of meerkats is in my head. And they're making a lot of noise. As if they're trying to kill one another. I think that's what meerkats do: kill the rellies.

The last thing I remember was Meg pouring me yet another glass of wine as I lay back on the bed. How did that happen? I was supposed to be the wine waiter.

Everything is garbled and fuzzy.

Meg is lying next to me on the bed. She is sliding her hands under the legs of my jeans (the wide ones) and massaging my ankles. I'm finding this very erotic. She's obviously the kind to take things slowly. She's taken off my boots. I'm pleased I'm lying down. She won't notice that I'm shorter than her with them off. She is naked except for her panties. And now she has moved up the bed and is kissing me. Her breasts are warm against my chest, and she is straddling me. She's a sylph, tiny, weightless apart from her breasts, which seem to swing around a lot. I want her to take my clothes off, but she obviously has her own playbook. I let her take charge. I like a woman in control. Next time I'll suggest she wears a nurse's uniform. She would look great in that. We could play doctors and nurses. I've read about that sort of thing. Women like to role play.

They like to pretend to be someone else. It gives them licence to do outrageous things. None of this happened. It is weird because I had Meg eating out of my hand. Everything was perfect: candles and Sibelius and champagne. We may have had too much to drink, but I'm thinking that was partly her fault. She seemed to be drinking way too fast. Was she trying to get me drunk so I would come on to her more? It's always hard to know. Girls are such a mystery. I'm still trying to figure them out. It's lucky that Meg is so into me because sometimes I get a bit overwhelmed with the stress of it all.

Next time I'll make sure to keep things under control. Maybe this is all for the best. Meg will be more relaxed on our second date. It's not as if there's any rush. We've got weeks. The coronavirus is making sure of that. I just need to be the man today. This is not going to be easy. For a start, I don't know exactly how last night ended. I've heard of people sending witty and disarming emails the morning after the night before, saying things like, *Is there anything I need to apologise for?* I have a better idea. I'll just play it by ear. Meg will be right there downstairs, and I will just *read* her. I'm very good at that. Intuitive.

But I need to get myself together. I go to the window to check the garden. I find I am doing this a lot these days, spying on my guests. It's not ideal, but I have to know what is going on without coming across as nosy or even interested. I have my own life, after all. And it's not about my paying guests. Roz is in the garden. She's sitting at the trestle, reading the paper. The sanitiser is on the table next to her. She's obviously got to it before Julius. Thank God. It's a perfect day, sunny with blue skies. Maybe I can suggest a walk with Meg later.

I'm thinking of just getting dressed and going downstairs. I open the bathroom cabinet and reach in for the hairspray. It's not where it usually is, and nor is the hairdryer. Actually, now I'm looking, most things are out of place as if someone has been in here searching for something. I should have expected that. Meg was in here last night. Several times. Fine, Meg, fine, it's okay if you want to root around in my bathroom. I don't know what you needed, but I know you meant well. You were trying to find something to make yourself fresh for the night ahead. I won't ask you anything. I'll pretend I didn't notice. Diplomatic: that's me.

I throw on my boots and good jeans and a new shirt: white linen. I want to look sharp, and the fabric bulks me up a little. At least I don't need to fiddle with my contact lens. I left it in last night. I should probably take it out and give my eye a rest, but I really want to see everything with crystal clarity today.

And then I remember the cat. Prince. He's been locked in the wardrobe all night. Christ.

Except he hasn't. The wardrobe door is ajar. Prince is nowhere to be seen, and Chelsea's bra is wedged in the jamb. He must have darted out when Meg left. I yank out the bra and slide back my clothes to check Chelsea's stuff. Her stilettoes are still at the back of the wardrobe, under my robe. Thank God for that. I search around for her panties. I hope to hell Prince got tired of them eventually and dropped them in the rafters or whatever. I need to get in there and check. But not now. I want to see Meg, get the lie of the land. I'm guessing she wouldn't have noticed the bra, not when she was so drunk and everything was so dark.

Roz has been at the whiteboard. She has drawn up two columns. They are headed CASES and DEATHS. Under CASES, she has written 541. Under DEATHS, she has written 1. Next to DEATHS, she has drawn a sad face.

Julius is on the phone. He's in a whole new get-up. Is this for Meg's sake, I'm wondering. If so, he's missed the mark. He's wearing a lime-green tee-shirt with *Later is Never* on the front, and shorts that are way too short, the type that was fashionable in the sixties when Kirk Douglas was prancing around on the silver screen amongst Roman emperors drunk on power and bad wine. He's the cross-dresser who can't decide which side of the fence to lean on.

He's in the garden doing circuits. Julius doesn't seem capable of thinking in a static position. It's as if he needs movement to get blood to his brain. You hear about that, don't you: advertising geeks who do headstands to flood their grey matter. When they're all fired up, completely engorged with serious rosea, they produce those jaunty jingles for Watties' peas or Heinz's Baked Beans that make you want to drive a pick through your brain.

Julius is not winning the argument. He looks as though he's just been offered some kind of plea-bargain, where the alternatives are not quite to his taste. Don't do it, Julius, I'm thinking. Be a man, not a mouse.

One thing I have to say about these garden conversations, apart from the obvious, which is that they are rather fun to listen to, is that Poppy is way more intelligent than Julius. And more articulate. She is definitely in control of Julius. And Julius is not up to the challenge.

'Why do you keep talking about string theory?' he is asking her. 'What's string theory got to do with anything? For God's sake, Poppy, I don't know where you're coming from.'

Poppy is a Maths graduate. I bet she knows exactly where she's coming from and can fully answer this simple question, which seems to have Julius on the ropes. I imagine it's her way of saying she's coming from planet Earth, and Julius is coming from another planet, so exponentially distant as to make any intelligible communication with normal people, such as her, completely impossible.

Well, she got that right.

And now Julius has gone for broke. 'Let me say something,' he is insisting. And Poppy must have decided to give him another chance because he has gone behind the shed and is talking fast and urgently. I can't make out what he is saying, but, whatever it is, I can tell that it's too long and very boring. And, worst of all, not pertinent. Julius has a tendency to whine and ramble. People don't want to hear a whole lot of drivel. Talking is not the same as saying something. Julius needs to learn this. Less is more—especially with language. The flab needs to go. Keep it simple and concrete. Be Churchillian. Someone really needs to sort Julius out. Soon.

There's no sign of Meg. She must be sleeping it off. I go out into the garden. Roz has created a cemetery next to her herb plot, I note. She's made a little cross out of twigs from her rosemary bush and set it into the soil. She's bent over the crossword.

'Evil, eleven letters,' she says, taking a drag on her cigarette without looking up.

'Malevolence,' I say.

'Mmm, maybe,' says Roz.

'Wickedness, then,' I say.

'Fits,' she says. She stubs out her cigarette and writes the letters in.

'Caress, six letters,' she says.

'Fondle,' I say immediately. I'm thinking of Meg.

'No, doesn't fit.'

'Stroke, then,' I say.

'How was it?' she asks as she writes it in.

'What?' I ask, although I know exactly what she's getting at.

'The big birthday bash,' says Roz, putting a lot of air into the words. She looks up from the newspaper. Her eyebrows are up. She's bursting to know. It's vicarious living at its worst. Some people just don't have lives. They rely on others to do all the living for them. She and Frank should get hitched. They would make an ideal couple.

'It was perfect.' I say. 'We might have drunk too many bottles of wine, but, hey, who's counting?'

'And the cake?' she asks.

'We didn't have time for that,' I say.

'Maybe I'll bring it back down then. I know Frank would like some.'

'I'll do that,' I say. I definitely do not want Roz back in my apartment.

'So someone has died in this country,' she says. 'That's the first of what will be many; you mark my words. There's all this talk about the girl from Lollipops, what's her name, Lily Lane or something. But what about that poor woman? She gets to a ripe and healthy old age only to be struck down by something completely beyond her control.'

'She was in her seventies,' I say and immediately regret it. I don't know how old Roz is, but she is clearly offended.

'Old lives matter, you know. They're people too,' she says. 'Boris will be next.'

'What?' I ask. I must admit I'm not really paying attention to Roz. I'm listening out for Meg.

'Boris Johnson, the British Prime Minister, has tested positive for the coronavirus. He's self-isolating at the White House.'

'I think you mean Number 10,' I say.

'So what's the latest, Roz?' asks Julius. He's off his phone at last. 'Anything about that dead girl?' He looks as though he has made some progress with Poppy. Good, maybe he'll leave Meg alone. He really needs to get that message loud and clear. It couldn't be more obvious that Meg thinks he's a loser.

'Yes, they've got a lead, apparently,' says Roz. 'There's a description here. They're looking for someone Caucasian of average height and build.'

'Well, that narrows things down,' says Julius. 'They've obviously got sweet F.A. It's a fishing expedition. The police these days, they're not trained. They clearly haven't the first clue.'

'Oh, let's send in Detective Inspector Julius Swann, then. Case closed.' I don't say this, but it's what Julius deserves. He really is a prat.

'There's a photo here,' says Roz, lighting another cigarette.

'What?' says Julius, bending over her. 'That's not a photo,' he says finally. 'It's an identikit. And it could be anyone. It's totally generic. Androgynous. It could be a woman. Look at all that hair. It's been curled and plumped up. It could be a wig. See what I mean.'

'Where's Meg?' I ask.

'Oh, she went out about an hour ago. She said she was going for a run,' says Roz. 'She looked as fresh as a bunch of daffodils in spring.'

CHAPTER FOURTEEN

SUNDAY 29th MARCH CONTINUED

Julius was right about the police because they are standing right outside Oak Tree Lodge. Roz is adamant that I check through the peep-hole before opening the door to anyone.

'You can't just let in any Tom, Dick and Harry,' she insists.

There are two of them. They look official. I'm thinking I need to let them in.

'It's the police,' I say to Roz. 'Here, see for yourself.'

'I don't care. And nor does the virus. Do you think the virus has any respect for a uniform? Do you think it even notices?'

I hope these are rhetorical questions because I can't think of an answer.

'No-one's immune, not even the police,' continues Roz. 'Especially not the police,' she adds. 'If they've been going door-to-door, then they're bound to be infected. They can't come in. That's definite.'

'You can't come in,' she shouts at the door. She's folded her arms.

'We have a few questions, Miss,' calls one of the policemen. 'It will only take a few minutes.'

'It only takes a few seconds to pass on the coronavirus,' Roz shouts back.

'What if we let them in and ask them not to touch anything? They can go out into the back of the garden, and we'll talk to them from the front,' I suggest.

'They're not coming inside,' screams Roz. 'Over my dead body.'

'If we don't let them in, it will look as though we are hiding something,' I say.

'I've got nothing to hide,' says Roz.

'What's going on?' says Frank. He's opened his bedroom door and is peering out. He looks as though he's just got up. He's wearing a grey robe, and his feet are bare. At least his hair is back in place; that's something. But he needs a shave.

'We're supposed to be socially distancing, and the police want to come inside,' says Roz.

'What do they want?' asks Frank. He's come out of his bedroom now, and there is a sweet smell about him, not sweet as in perfumed, but as in stale deodorant and old socks. Old unwashed socks.

'I don't know, and I care less,' says Roz firmly.

'We really need to talk to you,' raps the policeman.

'We have to let them in.' This is from Julius. 'They're just trying to do their job.' He's put his phone away and is carrying a clipboard. He's standing behind the reception desk.

'But nobody here knows anything,' says Roz.

'We don't know what we know. Sometimes people see things without realising it. It often happens. Someone holds the key to the mystery and is completely unaware of it.' Julius pulls his pen out of his pocket and writes something on his clipboard. He really is an insufferable prick.

'Is that right?' says Frank, who immediately goes back inside his bedroom and shuts the door.

'Open up!' shouts the policeman.

I need to get this situation under control before Meg gets back. Right now, it's looking as though Oak Tree Lodge is harbouring The Arcade Ripper. 'Officer,' I say, 'could you please meet us out back? You can go down the side of the house. We'll be happy to answer your questions in the garden.'

'Thank you, sir,' says the officer.

'Oh, God,' says Roz, snatching up the sanitiser.

'Come on, Roz,' I say. 'Don't make a fuss. Just follow behind me if you like.' Roz is squirting sanitiser on her hands and rubbing furiously. And now she's handing me the bottle and wanting me to do the same as if her conversation with the police has infected both of us.

I step outside, and Julius joins me. He holds his phone up and videos the two officers as they walk down the garden.

'Officers, do you mind going over there by the shed?' I call from the back door. Finally, Roz comes out and stands next to me. She has her arms folded in that Roz way that says, just piss off now and take your germs with you.

'Morning folks, I'm Sergeant Chambers, and this is Constable Banks. This will only take a few moments. It's as much for your benefit as ours.' They remove their hats as if to say, we're just being friendly: no need for alarm.

'What is that supposed to mean?' asks Roz urgently. She's reaching for her cigarettes.

'Is this everyone from the lodge?' asks the sergeant.

'Two missing,' I say. 'Meg Hart is out for a walk, and Frank is around here somewhere.'

'I'm here,' says Frank. He's got himself dressed and is in his wheelchair. He wheels himself outside.

'I'll just take your names, if I may,' says Sergeant Chambers. So far, Constable Banks hasn't said anything. Why is he even here, I'm wondering.

'I'm Julius, Julius Swann,' says Julius eagerly. 'Two n's in Swann,' he adds. I don't blame him for wanting to get that right. The name, Swann, well, it's not very blokey, is it? Actually, if you think about it, it's the exact opposite. It conjures up images of delicate necks and tutus and ballet shoes. Julius must have gone through life, starting at primary school, making sure everyone spelt his name with *two n's*. Imagine that. No wonder he's so fucked-up. He's lucky that Poppy has put up with him for so long.

'Roz Taylor,' says Roz. 'As in the film star,' she adds as if there can possibly be more than one way to spell her surname. I really need to sell up and get away from these people. A cuckoo's nest. That's what this place is turning into. Take the money and run. With Meg. We could make a life together. Her and me. Where is she?

'Frank Fisher,' says Frank.

Thank God for the simplicity of Frank.

'Leo Murdoch,' I say.

'And Miss Hart is out at the moment?' says the sergeant.

'Yes, but she shouldn't be too long,' I say.

'At this stage, enquiries are strictly routine. We just have one or two questions,' he says. Constable Banks nods at this, and the sergeant hands him the names he has just recorded. The constable pulls a pen from his shirt pocket. These guys look good in their uniforms. Navy blue, it's a fine colour. A strong, no-nonsense colour. I need to make it part of my dress code. It says, *I'm in charge*. It will suit me.

'We're here to make enquiries about the death of Janet Lane, which occurred sometime on Wednesday night or the early hours of Thursday, the first day of lockdown, to be precise. We would like each of you to account for your movements on that night.'

'I think I can save you a lot of time, sergeant, if I may speak for all of us,' I say. 'We take the lockdown very seriously. We are doing our bit, social distancing, sanitising, and basically staying home. So we were all here, all night, including Meg Hart. That's Hart as in the deer.'

'Is everyone happy if that goes on record?' asks Constable Banks. He looks across the garden at us. Roz says yes, and Julius and Frank are both nodding.

'Thank you,' says the sergeant. 'My only other question is to ask if anyone has seen anything out- of-the-ordinary, anyone unusual hanging around, any strange vehicles in the vicinity, anything at all that could help us with our enquiries.'

There is silence.

'It would help if you could tell us what you know,' says Julius. 'You know, sometimes background information can jog memories. We know the body was found in the arcade and that she worked for Lollipops, but that's all we know. How did she die? I mean, was she strangled or stabbed or shot? The newspapers aren't saying. Also, was she raped? Was there a sexual motivation? Was she robbed? Did she still have her purse with her? There are so many unanswered questions which would help in pushing the case forward. Was she drunk? Or drugged up?'

Julius finally comes to a halt. The two officers are eyeing each other. If I were them, I would place Julius under immediate arrest. There must be some ordinance that they can make stick. I hope they've got a straitjacket handy.

'I'm sorry, Mr Swann, but we can't jeopardise the progress of our enquiries by divulging any details. It's important not to contaminate the gathering of evidence. I'm sure you understand.'

It's clear that Julius does not understand because he's shaking his head and has his pen poised over his clipboard.

'The one thing we can divulge, in the interests of public health and in the interests of public safety, is that the deceased tested positive for the coronavirus. This is private information, normally kept private, but, as I'm sure you will appreciate, it has become even more important to identify the killer. Without knowing it, he or she is possibly spreading the virus. Becoming a super spreader. This makes it so much more vital that anyone with any information should come forward.'

Julius has a coughing fit, and everyone looks at him and moves away.

'For God's sake!' he says.

'Just get a test,' says Sergeant Chambers. 'Today,' he adds. 'Or Miss Lane may end up getting the last laugh.' And now the officers are replacing their hats and making their way up the garden.

Frank doesn't wait for them to leave. He's turned pale and wheels himself away to the bathroom. I guess he's the most at-risk in the house. He probably thinks he's already infected and won't survive.

'Julius, we're not saying you murdered Janet Lane,' says Roz reasonably.

This back-down, meant to calm Julius, has the polar opposite effect.

'Really?' screams Julius. 'Really?' he repeats. 'The mere fact that you have to say that is total bullshit.'

'All I'm saying is, just get a test. You need to be sure. You owe us that.'

'For fuck's sake,' says Julius.

'Think of Poppy,' I say. I don't for a moment think Julius is infected. He sneezes a lot. He's that type, allergic to everything, but I'm finding this summary diagnosis delicious.

'You spent a lot of time in the arcade, you know, sleuthing, mingling with the locals, the very people who would have spent time with Janet. Five degrees of separation and all that,' I say, doing my best to sound concerned.

'I don't think you should talk to Poppy until you've had the test,' says Roz definitively.

'For fuck's sake, Roz, the virus doesn't carry through smartphones. What you think it's part of electronics? Carried through air waves?' I think Julius should watch his language. Especially around Meg, even though she's not actually in the room right now.

'In point of fact,' I say, 'we don't know what this virus is capable of. You've heard what the medical chief says. Ashley Bloomfield reckons we don't know what we're dealing with. It's a very tricky virus. That's what he keeps telling us.'

'And we do know for a fact, Julius, actually, that it is airborne. That's a given. How can you not know that? Everyone knows that,' says Roz, pursing her lips.

Roz is always pursing her lips. It's a precursor for the next nicotine fix.

Julius has had enough. I don't blame him. He stalks from the room, and I can hear the front door as he slams it behind him.

CHAPTER FIFTEEN

MONDAY 30th MARCH

Food is dominating our lives. Eating is a comfort, but it's also a source of angst. Roz is our designated bubble shopper, as I think I've mentioned. She was delighted with the role at first. It gave her control of the virus. And us. But now she is terrified of going outside. The arcade murder hasn't helped. Stay home, stay safe, she keeps saying. Outside is where the hidden enemy lies in wait. She's watched that Cloverfield Lane movie too many times, the one where everyone stays in a bunker because the air outside is too toxic to breathe. She says no matter how careful she is when she goes out, she is putting herself in grave danger.

'And if I'm in danger, then so are all of you,' she says.

It's hard to argue with this. Julius doesn't bother to contribute to these discussions. He thinks they are beneath him. He's too busy working on his great opus. "Coronavirus, Up Close and Personal ", he's called it. Frank goes along with pretty much everything that Roz suggests.

So Roz has devised a new system. We will shop online and have everything delivered. This is good, in theory. Practice is another thing entirely. You have no idea how difficult it is for five people to come to an agreement on even what type of potatoes to put in the trolley: washed, unwashed, agria, red, perla; the list is endless. And it's the same with cheese and almost everything else. And then there is the question of quantities. No-one knows what two kilos of potatoes or tomatoes look like. We're used to buying half a bag or whatever, with no idea as to weight.

And then, when we finally get through to the checkout, Roz realises she's forgotten the broccoli. She's convinced that she's going to get cancer if she doesn't eat broccoli every day. Frank suggests that she should cut down on smoking. Roz is shocked by Frank's mutiny and flounces out of the room. We have to wait for her to compose herself and decide how many florets she needs.

And this is the easy part. After we've chosen and ordered and paid comes the real challenge: delivery. The whole point of the exercise is to have the food delivered, so no-one has to venture out into the great unknown.

And there are never any delivery times available. The only way to book a slot is to stay up until midnight and pounce when the week flips over to a new day.

This has become my job. I'm on my computer at midnight on shopping days. I say *shopping days*, but, actually, the delivery date is at least seven days away. Planning my meals on a daily basis is not that difficult. Trying to work out what I want to eat for seven days, in seven days' time, is doing my head in. Roz seems happy with lettuce and broccoli and the occasional radish to spice things up, Julius keeps insisting on barbecue food, sausages and the like, and Meg is too polite to make any requests (I'll eat anything is her mantra, why not my dick, then, I'm thinking) and Frank just goes with the flow.

The upside is I have an excuse to be downstairs on my laptop (in case of any last-minute requests) and can monitor Meg. She's a bizarre mixture of being either "on" in the way of celebrities or hiding in her bedroom. There doesn't seem to be any in-between.

And then, when the shopping arrives, delivered by an intrepid adolescent who looks as though he could flourish in a leper colony and win every challenge in *The Hunger Games*, Roz insists on taking charge. No-one is allowed to touch anything. We're not even permitted to help carry the items in. Everything is packed in paper carry-bags. Roz wears gloves. It's all executed with military precision. Newspapers are laid on the floor and bench in the kitchen before the shopping is brought in. This is all packaged up at the end and dropped in the recycling bin along with the carry-bags and gloves. Roz was washing everything before, a sort of *eco rinse* operation, but now the dial is definitely turned right round to *deep wash*. She's our Sherpa, guiding us across the mountainous ridges and spurs of pestilence and plague. I suppose I should be grateful.

The other thing that is dominating our lives is the police visit. Roz is convinced the police think we're implicated somehow because we live in a boarding house.

'People are coming and going here; we can't keep track of things,' says Roz. 'That's why they're giving us a hard time. That's why they insisted on taking our names and asking so many questions.'

'Mostly going,' says Frank.

'What do you mean by that?' I ask.

'Chelsea went,' says Frank.

'For God's sake, Frank,' I say, 'there's very little turnover here, as you well know. And their questions were merely routine.' I want to add something along the lines of, *more's the pity*, but I bite my tongue.

Meg is playing hard-to-get. She's been coy ever since the birthday dinner. More than coy, she's been elusive. I think she's worried about having rushed things in the beginning. I need to respect that. You have to respect girls. Play along, be the man, while playing the wimp. It's a fine line to walk. You somehow have to pretend you're completely okay with being on a total promise and then being let down. Meg is an outrageous flirt. But that's okay. She's really very shy, and it's all part of her courtship ritual. I get it. I get it, Meg; I really do. I'm expected to read the signals and take charge. But where are you? I haven't seen you this morning. Are you doing yoga in your room? Come out, come out, wherever you are.

I'm spending too much time fraternising with my guests. They get on my nerves at the best of times. But what else can I do? Obviously, I would like to be able to phone Meg or send her an email and ask her out. That would be normal. But these are extraordinary times. The Prime Minister and everyone else, for that matter, keep banging on about *the new normal*. The new normal for me is loitering downstairs in the kitchen in the hope that Meg will emerge from her room and need a glass of water or something.

And when I'm not downstairs, I'm doing the next best thing that allows me to monitor things (apart from using my wardrobe peep-hole), and that is keeping vigil from my window. This can be very tedious. Who wants to watch that scrawny Roz watering her herbs and waving bluebottles away from her compost heap? It's a downer. The trouble is, I'm hooked. I'm the drug addict who's run out of baggies and is desperate for a fix. So here I sit. It's nearly lunchtime. Meg usually puts on a matinée performance, a late matinée sometime just before noon.

And here she is, walking out into the garden in yet another come-and-get-me outfit. I can see her clearly from my window. She's sporting a two-piece arrangement, bright yellow, and is carrying a huge straw hat and shades. She looks like something out of a James Bond movie. They're my favourite films. The guy always gets the girl. And it's always on his terms. After the raunchy (and elegant) sex scene, he vaults into his Aston Martin, scales a vertical drawbridge, lands with the finesse of a pilot, and, with the wind tousling his hair, races along the perilously narrow Amalfi Coast road.

Meg is swinging a towel (a bath towel, the one I gave her from Cranberry's when she arrived) and a book. She's laying out the towel on the grass. And she's got some suntan lotion. She spends some time arranging herself as if playing to the gallery. Which, of course, is exactly what she is doing. She knows I'm up here in my eyrie looking down at her.

It's very hot up here. There's a drift of air through the window, which is cooling my chest. And my head, thank God: I don't want my hair to collapse. But not my groin. I need to get my jeans off. Denim is a very hot fabric; it doesn't breathe. I need to breathe. I really need to sort myself out and my wardrobe. I've become more aware of this since Meg arrived. Fixing my wardrobe is a mission because all the shops are closed. Online purchasing and delivery are allowed under level four, but I'm not confident about choosing the right thing from a website. What you see is never what you get, a bit like girls.

I really haven't got time to get my boots off. So I just undo my fly and ease everything down. It feels good. It's cooler, and I'm less confined. I really need a bit more room. I step away from the window a little. I don't want to be seen.

And suddenly Julius appears out of nowhere. He's wearing white cargoes. No shirt. And some gold-rimmed shades, the type you see in the $2.00 shop a few doors down. I have to admit Julius is ripped. I haven't noticed this before, but I'm noticing it now. And so is Meg because she's looking up at him from her towel. She's lying on her stomach in that Marilyn Monroe pose with her calves pointing to the sky and crossed at the ankles. Her book is open on the grass in front of her, and she's got her forefinger holding the book open in case she loses her place, which seems to be page one.

And now Julius, without so much as a by-your-leave, is flopping down next to Meg on the grass. I'm sorry, Meg, I'm thinking. I'm so sorry that Julius is such a buffoon. Please don't judge me by my lodgers.

Watching Julius is a bad vibe. I'm no longer feeling squashed up. If anything, I'm feeling the opposite, as if the universe is too big for me. I yank my jeans up. I really need to get some more meds. I believe I can just phone through a prescription request to my medical centre and pick it up at reception, which is right next to a pharmacy. They're all considered essential services. And that's exactly what they are. Essential. Especially in my case.

And suddenly Julius has jumped up in the nimble way of little guys and headed inside. Thank God. Meg has obviously asked him to give her some space. I need to get myself together and make it clear to Julius that he's persona non grata. That's if he's even heard that phrase. I bet he hasn't. He's a complete ignoramus. Another word that's probably not in his personal thesaurus.

And now he's back with two glasses of wine, and Meg is smiling her solar smile at him and taking the glass. She is moving over so that Julius can lie next to her, and there is only one thought going through my head: *Julius needs to disappear.* Just like Chelsea. He's pointing to Meg's book and pretending to take an interest. Actually, it's giving him an opportunity to scope out Meg's cleavage and side-boob. Her top is on the skimpy side and definitely offers no support. Her breasts are out of control. What do they call it? A wardrobe malfunction? There are serious wardrobe malfunctions going on here right now, and Julius is the beneficiary of all of them.

And now Meg hands him the book, and I can clearly hear her saying, 'Tell me what you think. I'd really like your take on it.'

I don't want to hear Julius's take on Meg's book. I need a glass of water. I go to my kitchen and imagine Julius nodding and looking serious as he tries to mind-fuck Meg. He's a walking aneurysm about to burst.

He really needs to go.

I'm back at the window. And the conversation seems to have morphed into the topic of Chelsea's whereabouts. I get right up close to the window and strain to hear.

'Was she really unhappy?' says Meg.

'I think she was,' says Julius.

What the hell would he know?

'I mean, not just about her job, about her life in general,' says Meg.

'I never really took much notice,' says Julius. I can tell he wants to change the subject and talk about himself. That's his go-to topic.

'How do you think she fitted in here?' asks Meg.

I'm wondering why Meg is so interested in Chelsea. I guess that's just her: kind and considerate and full of compassion. Come up here, Meg and be kind and considerate and compassionate to me.

'It's really hard to say. I'm not sure she liked Leo very much. She did her best. She was friendly and pleasant, but I felt she was just tolerating him. You know, like laughing at his jokes and flattering him, but, all the while, holding her nose.'

WTF, I'm thinking, and then Julius's phone is going, and it must be Facetime because he is rolling away from Meg. It is clearly too late because he has that look on his face as if he's been taken to the principal's office and is hoping for a black hole to come along and swallow him up.

'She's nobody,' says Julius.

Oh, here we go. Poppy again. Delicious.

That Poppy must have a set of lungs on her because Julius is holding the phone away from him again.

'What do you mean, I need to get a test? She's clean,' replies Julius, throwing Meg a look of apology. And now Poppy must be treating Julius to a Dr Ashley Bloomfield lecture because Julius is silent for some minutes.

'Well, I don't know for sure, but I'm pretty sure,' he says lamely. And then he disappears behind the shed and becomes blessedly inaudible.

CHAPTER SIXTEEN

MONDAY 30th MARCH CONTINUED

Roz went outside earlier. Not just outside, as in the back garden for a smoke. She has left Oak Tree Lodge. She is in the street. She smoked a lot of cigarettes before she left and was sipping at a glass of wine. Not to be judgemental, but I think it's pertinent to mention that this was before the sun was over the yard arm, as they say in nautical circles. She was sitting in her racing green rocking-chair.

Before she left, she said, 'Everything is driving me nuts.'

There was a lot I could have said in response to this, but I kept my counsel. There's often a downside to letting people inside your head.

And now she is back. She's in the kitchen sanitising with the newspaper tucked under her arm.

'Wow, it's crazy out there,' she says.

'How so?' I ask, trying to sound interested.

'People are stepping off the pavement onto the road to get away from everyone else. There aren't any cars. It's as if we've stepped back in time as if we've travelled back to the nineteenth century.'

'Except there are no horse-drawn carriages,' I say.

Roz glares at me. 'There is a queue to get into the supermarket. Someone is standing outside and monitoring people's entry. It's strictly one at a time. It's

like nothing I've ever seen before, except in movies. I went down into the park to have a sit-down, and all the benches are chained up, so you can't use them. People are lying on the grass on blankets. And you can't get into the public loo. There's a padlock on the door.'
'That padlock has been there forever,' I say. 'But chaining up seating is weird. You'd think it would be the safest place in the world, a park bench in the open, in the fresh air,' I say.
'The powers-that-be don't want people congregating. The park is a magnet for all sorts, mainly drifters and homeless people. Two strangers sitting on a wooden bench is a recipe for disaster.' This is a pearl from Julius, who seems to be spending a lot of time in the living room these days. Far too much time. Roz moves away from him and seats herself at the end of the dining able.
'And there were teddy bears in windows,' she continues. 'Made me cry. People doing that: it's something, isn't it? It's a signal. It's kindness; that's what it is. Our PM keeps on telling us to be kind, doesn't she? I guess kids are having a tough time too. Easter's coming up. There won't be any egg hunts. Can't even drive your kids to the beach.'
'It's insane,' says Julius.
'Have you had a test yet?' asks Roz sharply.
'I have, as it happens,' says Julius. 'Poppy was worried.'
'So you have to self-isolate,' says Roz. 'Maybe, you should go and stay with Poppy.'
'Are you out of your mind?' says Julius. 'I'm supposed to stay in my bubble; that's the whole point.'
'So it's okay to infect all of us, but not Poppy.'

'Look, it's too late now, and anyway, what are the chances?' says Julius.

Roz picks up the thermometer and the sanitiser. She places them on the edge of the dining table and then stalks out to the garden. She's feeling for her cigarettes as she goes. She keeps them in the front pocket of her blouse, nice and handy.

'I'd say the chances are pretty high, actually, Julius,' I say. 'You've been up close and personal with all those junkies from the arcade, gathering evidence and God-knows-what else in the process.'

I love the idea of Julius being confined to his room for so many reasons, mainly because it keeps him away from Meg and clears the decks. He is a distraction. More than a distraction, he's an obstacle. He's ruining everything.

'For Christ's sake,' says Julius. 'Fine, fine, I'll do it. The results are due back tomorrow morning. I'll self-isolate until then. I need some space anyway,' he adds. 'There's way too much noise around here. It's hard to concentrate on anything meaningful.'

'Why don't you try one of those flotation tanks, you know, once you're in the clear.'

'What?' asks Julius.

'You know, you lie in a pool filled with water with only silence for company. It revs up the creative neurons, and you come out feeling like Einstein, or maybe Shakespeare, in your case.'

I have Julius's attention. I can tell he is considering this. Excellent. I'm hoping he opts for the one in South Auckland, where the attendants routinely forget to alert clients the session is over, and the automatic filtration system kicks in with life-threatening results. I heard about a girl who got her hair tangled up and had to have it (what was left) shaved off. Imagine it: Julius bald. Delicious. It wouldn't suit him at all.

He's on his phone again. I hope he's making a booking. I read somewhere recently that too much time on devices destroys the elasticity of the brain and basically makes it impossible to focus on things. Julius could put himself forward for whatever study scientists are working on. He's the perfect example of anecdotal evidence proving this theory beyond any doubt.

As far as I'm concerned, things are progressing far too slowly. I need a fix. Specifically, I need a Meg fix. She led me on, and then she let me down. I can't get the image of Meg in her skimpy bikini, lying next to Julius and drinking wine in the garden (my garden), out of my mind.

So I'm in my wardrobe again. Meg is in the shower. I saw her go in. She knows how the taps work now, so I won't have much time. I promised myself I wouldn't do this, but sometimes when I talk to myself, my brain doesn't listen. I haven't bothered with Sibelius (I need to find some different music) or Chelsea's bra. I don't want to think about her right now. I've slid down my jeans. They're always way too tight at times like these.

It's just you and me, Meg.

She reached in and turned the hot tap right around. Well done, Meg, you're a quick study.

And now she's stepping in.

Oh, Meg, you're sunburnt. You've got thin, white strap marks on your shoulders and back. And your breasts are sheet-white against your lobster front. You really copped it. Your shoulders are crimson. You're going to peel.

It's your own fault. You should have known better. You're not in London now. New Zealand has a big hole in its ozone layer. How could you not know this? UV rays are a killer here. I would have looked after you. You had suntan cream. I would have rubbed it on you. I would have massaged it all over you with love and attention to detail. And then I would have reapplied it after thirty minutes or whatever it says on the tube.

The water is too hot on your hot skin, and you're turning on the cold tap. Perfect. There's less steam, and my peep-hole is not fogging up as much. I can relax. I've got plenty of time to enjoy the entertainment. I'm sorry it has to be this way, Meg, but I bought tickets for your birthday party, and the show got cancelled. You owe me, and I'm collecting.

Meg grabs the soap and rubs it between her hands. This is the part I am looking forward to, the part where she rubs herself. It's a turn-on to watch a girl touching herself, almost as good as the real thing. It looks as though Meg's standing on tip toes while she does this, stretching her body, elongating it, a kind of yoga pose. She looks all willowy and fragile, as if she wants company, someone to wash her back or something. I'm imagining getting her up against the wall of the shower. That's obviously what she wants, someone to take charge.

And now Meg has stopped sudding up and is rinsing the soap off her hands under the nozzle and turning off the shower. She is reaching out through the curtain and picking something up off the floor. It's her phone. It's ringing. She swipes it and says, 'Hello, Meg Hart.' She's all business as if she's talking to a complete stranger. Or someone important.

Who answers the phone like that, I'm wondering. Someone who is trying to impress the person on the other end is who. I need to know who Meg is trying to impress. I turn my head to the side and press my ear to my peep-hole. The trouble is I did such a good job of the installation that everything is pretty much sound-proofed. This was very important. I didn't want anyone in the shower to hear what was going on in my apartment.

I can't make out what Meg is saying. She's lowered her voice. All I can get is a sense of tone. It's urgent and serious. And then Meg steps out of the shower. I can't see her anymore. What's going on, Meg? What can be so important that you're interrupting your shower? You're putting your unwashed, sunburnt skin back into your clothes when what you should be doing is finishing up and moistening with an after-sun cream. I will help you with this. I would help you with the hard-to-reach places.

This must be important, somebody important. Who can it be? Who can it possibly be? I'm disappointed in you, Meg. You're a bit more complicated than you seem. Are you hiding things from me? Do I need to come downstairs and find out what you are up to? Yes, I think I do. I've hardly seen you since your birthday. You're either in your room or out jogging or whatever you do when you leave the house.

I need a shower. I seem to have made a mess of myself, and my hair is matted to my scalp. I can't remember a hotter summer. We're experiencing record temperatures according to the met office. There's a lot of talk about the weather these days. Scientists are speculating about the coronavirus. Heat is supposed to slow down transmission, so we must be thankful. I'm finding it hard to be thankful when I'm dripping with sweat. I need to dry off and cool down. I get myself out of the wardrobe and strip off my shirt. I stand by the window and let the air flow do its work. I'm not sure how much time I've got if I want to catch Meg, but I can't let her see me like this.

It's all taken too long. Getting my hair back in place, even without washing it, seems to be taking longer and longer. By the time I'm ship-shape, Meg has gone. I get to the bottom of the stairs just as she is leaving. I catch a glimpse of her back as she closes the door. She's wearing that black dress again, the one where the straps keep falling down. And she's got her hair loose.

That's never a good sign. Well, depending on where you sit. Hairstyles are very much like shoes. There are sexually active shoes and sexually inactive shoes. Stilettoes, for example, tell the observer that the wearer is *up for it on a daily basis*. Crocs, well, not so much. It's the same with hair. A low ponytail tied at the nape means *I'm unavailable: fuck off.* Hair flowing long and free, especially if it's blond, is a loudhailer blaring *let's go to bed right now, and the kitchen bench will do nicely.*

So who is Meg fucking? I really need to know. I race to the door and crack it open. She's crossed the road. A car is pulling up. She's going round to the kerbside and climbing in the back. I can't see who's in the driver's seat. The person is turned towards Meg. But I can be certain of one thing: it's a guy, a big guy. And then the car speeds away.

CHAPTER SEVENTEEN

MONDAY 30th MARCH CONTINUED

I stole a hat today.

After Meg left the lodge, I left too. I went down the road, socially distancing, of course. I'm a responsible citizen. I'm doing my bit, keeping our bubble safe. I stuck to the road. It was just as busy on the pavements. We're allowed to go out and about as long as we stay within four kilometres of home.

It wasn't a great hat, I have to admit. It's hard to steal high-ticket items with everything in lockdown. Usually, when I get these urges, I lose myself in the big department store at the end of the street. It's easy-peasy in there. No-one pays any attention, and you've pretty much got the run of the place. The only challenge is to be decisive. You can't appear to be loitering. A lot of people do loiter in here. Street folks come in to covet things they can't afford or just to get warm. So it's easy to be invisible. There are CCTV cameras. I look out for them. But I've come to the conclusion that unless someone is actually mugged in the aisles, no-one will bother to check the footage.

Just to be clear, I don't do this sort of thing all that often. Not these days, anyway. And I'm really trying to stop. But sometimes Mr Mad just comes thumping at the door of my head. When it's a gentle rap, I can screen him out. But today, after I was watching Meg in her hat in the garden, he just wouldn't go away. I'm beginning to wonder if Meg is worth it. I know she wants me, and I don't mind a girl playing the game, but there are limits.

My counsellor told me it's important to know where you're going in life, especially with friendships. Friends can be put into two categories, she said: those who bring you down and those who lift you up. Sometimes friendships are all one way. You are doing all the giving, and they are doing all the taking. My counsellor said there had to be a return on your investment. She used to talk a lot like that. Money and percentages and outlay. She was very commercial. She should have been an accountant. She looked like an accountant: thin lips, hair scraped back in a tight bun, and rimless glasses. She wasn't very sexy. And she wasn't motherly either. A counsellor should be one or the other, I reckon. Otherwise, what's the point?

I only went once.

Meg, I'm happy to do things for you, give you the best towels in the house, make you a beautiful birthday dinner, and treat you to champagne, but what am I getting in return? In the cold light of day, I'd have to say, not a lot. Let's see, so far, we've only been on one date. It was nice and all the rest. But you ran out on me, Meg. When the going got hard (no pun intended), you went AWOL. Not only that, you flirted with Julius. You lay with him on my towel in my garden. You're going to have to lift your game. And what about the phone call and the mystery car driver? I'm prepared to give you the benefit of the doubt for now. You might have been getting into an Uber for an essential errand. You might have been going across town (forbidden) for something life-and-death. Maybe you had an urgent doctor's appointment that you were waiting to have confirmed by phone. I'll let you have that. But, at some stage, you're going to have to prove it.

About the hat.

Here's what happened. It was mid-afternoon when I got to the shop. It's a chemist shop. Pharmacies are allowed to be open. They're in the category of providing essential services under level four. People have to have their heart pills, their paracetamol, and their cough mixture. But the thing is, chemists are no longer dedicated. They have extended their range of merchandise so that they're mini-supermarkets, not quite up to the Walmart that you find on every street corner in New York, where they sell pharmaceuticals, but also wine and sandwiches and nuked sausages and meatballs, and a lot else besides. Pharmacies have pushed the envelope. They sell all sorts of shit that is not even close to essential: candles, diffusers, perfume, and even jewellery. If they were more community-minded and safety-conscious, they would cordon off this stuff that the whole world can do without even under level one. Or is it level none? I think normality is level none. The new normal is zero. Think of that.

I didn't even have to go inside the shop. The hats are placed outside on a stand so that passers-by can't miss them. A bit like the chocolate and mind-numbing magazines stationed at the check-out of supermarkets. These are in the category of impulse buys, which just goes to prove my point. How can anything you buy on impulse be in the category of essential? So these places really bring it on themselves. This stuff is shoved right under your nose. It's worse than that; it's actually cluttering up the entrance to the shop; it's in the way; it's an obstacle to be navigated. What do the shop owners expect?

Let the record show I took only one hat. I could have taken a whole bunch of them because they were in a stack. It would have been just as easy to lift the lot. But, no, Mr Mad, I took only one. It was an effort. I had to lever the top one off the pile. I held it in my hands, casual-like, and then I simply folded it in two and shoved it in my carry-bag. I was not even sure what the colour was when I stole it.

On my way home, I pass Ozzy. He's in his usual place at the entrance to the arcade. This is not working for him these days. It's normally a thoroughfare, the busiest place in the area, with people passing by and going in and out. But with everything closed, very few people are going into the arcade. I don't suppose the recent murder has helped. *The body in the arcade* is the phrase on everyone's lips. There are plenty of walkers taking their exercise, but they're giving him a wide berth. He's doubly disadvantaged. He could be infected with the coronavirus, and he looks none-too-clean as if he could be harbouring some other contagion.

It's very hot again today, and Ozzy has his shirt buttons undone. He's got a wonderful tattoo of a New Zealand fern on his chest. It covers the whole of his right pec. He wears it well. The tattoo artist has taken advantage of the curve of Ozzy's musculature, which is considerable. As usual, he's got his sign laid out on the pavement. It's in very small print and hard to read.

It says: *My name is Ozzy, King of Kings, Look on my works, ye mighty and despair.* And then he's added a smiley face. The friendliness of the face is supposed to make up for the arrogance of the poem, I guess.

The mighty works he's referring to are his sole possessions. He's actually got quite a lot of gear. There's a sleeping bag, clothing, a fold-up canvas chair, and a supermarket trolley. Also, a metal fan that looks very old. I often wonder about his fan. I don't think it's battery-operated. Maybe there are electrical outlets in the arcade or wherever. Who knows?

Ozzy is a very handsome man. He has fine skin, for a start, swarthy and smooth. And a boxer's build. Some people are just blessed. I'm pretty sure Ozzy has done nothing to earn his good looks except drink too much vodka. He's very tall as well, a giant of a man. So normal folks, those who live in houses and have jobs and regular pay checks and ugly faces and hobbit bodies (like Julius), can feel good about themselves when they drop a coin in his tin. He may be an Adonis, but what good has it done him, they are thinking with satisfaction when they flick a crumb his way.

Ozzy told me once about the stuff written on his cardboard. It was composed by a great thinker who died young. Ozzy used to be an English teacher way back when. I don't think his poem is helping his cause. *Between jobs, please help* would work a whole lot better in my view. But sometimes there's no telling people, especially people like Ozzy, who have their pride, after all.

I spot him fifty bucks. I can afford this. And it makes me feel good.

'God bless,' he says. Automatic. He doesn't look up.

Normally, I would hunker down next to him and shoot the breeze. But I'm following the rules, and, I must admit, I'm keen to get my stash off the streets.

But I want his take on the death of Janet Lane. I'm wondering what he knows about this. If anyone has the goods on what went down, it will be Ozzy. He knows everyone, and even with a bottle of vodka on board, he's more clear-eyed and logical than most people. Certainly, he would run rings around Julius. Julius has been here playing detective with his clipboard, but I bet he hasn't interviewed Ozzy. The first thing any journalist needs to learn is how important your sources are. A journalist has to develop relationships with people in the know. It's all about contacts and protecting them. Julius has no finesse. No-one will ever trust him, and he doesn't have the nous to recognise the real deal when he sees it. Ozzy isn't white, and he's not wearing a suit, so Julius wouldn't bother talking to him.

Ozzy has no time for Julius. He calls him a lightweight. Ozzy is like that, polite and euphemistic. What he really means is Julius is a fuckwit.

'Hey, Ozzy,' I say, crouching down a metre away.

'Hey, yourself,' replies Ozzy, looking up at me with his wide, brown eyes and megawatt grin.

'So what do you know?' I ask.

'Folks are going crazy around here, is what,' he says.

'You got that right,' I say.

'Really crazy,' he repeats. 'They're scared of the wrong things.'

'What do you mean?' I ask.

'There's killing going on.'

'Did you know Janet?' I ask.

'Everyone knew Janet,' he says. 'She was a lovely girl. Too nice for her own good.'

'What happened?' I ask.

'She got murdered,' says Ozzy. 'That's all I know.'

'Did you ever see her,' I ask, 'you know, to speak to and spend some time with?'

'Sure, she hung out with everyone. Everyone knew Janet. She was a looker. The police have questioned everyone. They have a shit load of info but no real leads. Not yet, anyway. Shame, folks are scared enough without this. Gives the place a bad name.'

'Anything you need, Ozzy?' I ask.

'I got everything I need,' he says, leaning back against the wall of the arcade and closing his eyes.

'See you, then,' I say. I push myself up and walk away. I need to get home.

'Frank knew her too,' calls Ozzy after me. 'Ask him.'

I look back at Ozzy and give him a wave. I'm not surprised to hear this. I don't monitor Frank's comings and goings, but Roz bangs on about his late-night jaunts. I've got more important things on my mind than the movements of a bald, old man in a wheelchair. Right now, it's the hat in my carry-bag.

And now I've got it home, I'm having a good look at it. I've taken it out of my bag and unfolded it. It's yellow, the colour of a canary. It's also quite floppy with a wide brim. It's woven. I look at the label: *made in China*, $29.95. That's not a lot of money, not a big score. But it's an okay hat. I put it on. In the bathroom: I don't want to be seen through my bedroom window. I pull the brim down at the front in the way that actresses do in movies set in Cannes. It really is a very chic hat, I'm thinking. Maybe I'll give it to Meg as a belated birthday present. It would suit her. It would be my way of saying, it's okay, Meg, I forgive you for your transgressions.

Maybe I could persuade her to put her two-piece on when she next visits. Then I could get her to model it for me. A golden hat on my golden girl. That would be something.

CHAPTER EIGHTEEN

TUESDAY 31st MARCH

The bell is ringing at reception. I'm in my apartment, and I can hear it clearly without Roz yelling up the stairs. How can she not know that? And then I hear another voice.

'Open up. It's Quentin.'

I run downstairs. Roz is standing by the entrance with her forefinger to her lips.

'Just stay quiet. We don't have to let him in,' she says. 'He's not the police.'

'For God's sake, Roz,' I say, 'I'm not going to hide inside my own house. And isn't it a little late for that?'

Roz grabs my arm. She's surprisingly strong, and her nails are digging into my skin.

'Just stay quiet,' she repeats, 'and he'll go away.'

I'm considering my options. Maybe Roz has a point. Quentin was not exactly calm during the last visit. Do I need this? There's been the nasty business of the death in the arcade. I know Quentin. He'll be reading a whole lot into it, extrapolating and coming up with the wrong conclusions. He should spend some time with Julius. They would be best buddies. They have a lot in common: both more than a little on the hysterical side, equally narcissistic and entitled, and it would be a coin-flip to decide who is the more apocalyptically brain-dead.

When this is all over, maybe I'll invite Quentin over for a sausage sizzle and leave them to it.

'Are you expecting someone?' Quentin is standing behind us in reception. He's come down the side of the house and walked in. He's got his usual bullshit gear on: over-dressy trousers, business shirt (offices are closed, Quentin; didn't you get the memo?) and shoes and socks (WTF?).

'You need to sanitise,' hisses Roz. 'You shouldn't be in here. How dare you barge in here, into our bubble? You have no right.' She moves to the front door and flattens herself against it.

'I want to know what happened to Chelsea,' says Quentin.

'Question already asked and answered,' says Roz. She reads a lot of John Grisham. I'm pretty sure that's the line of one of his hot-shot lawyer characters, more than one of his hot-shot lawyer characters: Grisham is very repetitive. It sets Quentin off.

'There's something not right here,' he shouts. 'Something smells, something smells very bad, and it's right here in this bullshit lodge with its fancy fretwork and bullshit pleather seats.'

I'm pretty offended by Quentin's insults, but I keep it together. Temper tantrums solve nothing.

'Look, Quentin,' I begin.

'No, you look, mate,' interrupts Quentin, and he's closing in on me. Roz squeals and darts away from the door, taking refuge in the hallway. 'There's no way Chelsea would have left without letting me know. She just wasn't like that. I don't believe that you don't know anything. You're hiding something.'

'Have you quite finished?' I ask.

Quentin has begun that bouncing on his toes again. And sweat is pouring off him. He's one of those moist types with no control over his body functions at the best of times, but especially not when the going gets tough. Which is now.

'The police have been here. They've taken our statements, and they're satisfied. Okay? I'm not quite sure what you want from us, Quentin. There's really nothing else to say.'

'And I'd like to point out,' says Roz, 'that you're breaking the law just by being here. You're not supposed to be breaking our bubble. We're in lockdown.' Roz has her arms folded again. 'It's level four,' she adds as if the whole of New Zealand doesn't know.

'And what about that other girl, Janet Lane?' asks Quentin. He has left his mouth open at the end of this sentence, and there is spittle on his tongue. Not a good sign.

'What about her?' I ask.

'What do the police think about that?'

'How should I know?' I say.

'Have the police been here?'

'Look, Quentin, the police visited as part of their routine inquiries. They interviewed every one of us, and they went away satisfied.'

'Don't you find it odd that not one, but two girls living within a kilometre of each other are unaccounted for?' asks Quentin.

'We know what happened to Janet. She was murdered,' says Roz. 'At least, that's what the news reports are implying.'

I don't think Roz is helping the situation. Quentin snaps his head in her direction, and it looks like the motherboard of his brain has shut down, like there's been some kind of short circuit or something.

And then there is a plaintive miaow, and, out of nowhere, Prince is rubbing himself around my ankles.

Quentin looks down at the cat and then looks away. And then he looks back down, and I can hear the fizz and crackle of a serious reboot in his cranium.

'What the fucking fuck!' he yells. 'That's Chelsea's cat. That's Chelsea's cat,' he repeats.

'Prince, yes, it is,' I say mildly, trying to calm the waters. 'Chelsea left him behind when she went. I've been looking after him, you know, feeding him until she comes back to collect him.'

'I think he's missing Chelsea,' coos Roz. 'Sad, really,' she adds, shaking her head.

I really wish Roz would go out into the garden and sit in her rocking-chair and water her yucca or whatever and let me deal with this.

'What the fuck is wrong with you people?' screams Quentin. 'Chelsea would never have left Prince behind. She adored that cat. She talked about him all the time. He was her baby. What the bloody fuck!' Quentin has balled his fists up and is screwing them into his eyes as if to erase the existence of Prince.

'Look, mate, how do you know what Chelsea would have done? You can't possibly know. She was obviously going through a tough time. People act out of character sometimes,' I say.

'What the fuck would you know about anything, Leo? You're a fucking freak show. Take a look in the mirror sometime. You're a fucking gargoyle. You belong up there on your fancy gables, scaring off whatever, whatever the fuck, who knows? Whatever it is, it would definitely work in your case.'

I'm more than a little taken aback by this tirade and am formulating a suitably cutting takedown when Quentin grabs Prince and makes for the front door.

'I'm going to the police!' he yells. 'I'm going to have everyone in this godforsaken funny farm arrested.' And with that, he flings open the door and strides out.

'Did you know that we're shedding cells at the rate of a thousand a second?' screams Roz, grabbing the sanitiser. She makes for the front door and squirts the handle.

'I did not know that, Roz,' I say.

'Well, it's true, a scientific fact.' She's waving the sanitiser about as she says this. 'We need to get a gate for the side garden, a barrier, something to stop people from just barging in.' Roz reaches into her pocket and grabs her packet of cigarettes. She draws one out and jabs it into her mouth. She's looking at her watch. Is it too early for a wine, she's thinking. Obviously not, because she retreats down the hallway, and I can hear her wine fridge tinkling as she opens it.

I am thinking *hell is other people*. How can I make them all disappear? Roz, Frank, Quentin and Julius, especially Julius. But not Meg. I'll make an exception for Meg. For now.

I haven't seen her since she disappeared into the mystery vehicle. I don't even know if she came home last night. If she didn't come back, then we have a problem, Houston. First of all, it means she is breaking the rules of our bubble. But, more importantly, she's two-timing me. And I can't have that. It's not that I'm possessive, and I'm not the jealous type, but fair's fair.

I need to know what is going on. Is that unreasonable? I'm not sure how to find out, but I'm thinking the only way is to have a look in her room. I'm no snoop; that's not me. But I think I have a right. Someone needs to be in charge here. I own the place, after all.

I grab the spare key to Meg's room, Chelsea's old room. I knock gently first. I wait two minutes and knock again. I give her another two minutes and then unlock the door and push it open.

This girl is disciplined: everything is as neat as a pin. Her bed is beautifully made-up with hospital-cornered sheets. Oh, Meg, we could be such a team. I love your standards. Your pillows are straight and plumped up on the bed. You obviously value your bed, as if it's an important part of your life. I like that. And there are no clothes lying around. Everything is in its place. You have even hung up your towels on the back of the door. You're a detail person. You're organised and orderly. Not like Chelsea. I just know this relationship is going to work. The sash window is partially open so that the room is fresh, the smell of disinfectant gone, and the rug no longer musty. It really is a beautiful room: the pressed steel ceiling is a work of art with its embossed rondel of roses and grapes and cherubs. I imagine myself lying on the coverlet with you, Meg, looking up at it. You really are the perfect lodger. Normally absence is to be prized. The ideal tenants pay their rent and never show up. But in this case, a little company would be welcome, more than welcome. Where are you, Meg?

It's hard to tell anything from the room. I would like to know what Meg's wearing. Is she still in the little black dress? This would be a clue. If it's in the wardrobe, then she came back yesterday and changed into something else. This is vital information. It would tell me if she stayed out all night or not. I would really like to know what's in her wardrobe anyway. Clothes maketh the man, isn't that the saying? It must also apply to the woman.

I'm about to open the wardrobe door when I see the book she was showing Julius yesterday in the garden. She's left it on the bedside table. I recognise it because it's an unusual colour: lime green. I need to check the title, maybe get my own copy on Kindle and read it. It would be a conversation filler. I could say something like: 'Hey, I know that book; it's my favourite,' or something. Girls like boys who read. It makes them feel safe.

I scoop up the book and flick through it. It's a thin volume and it's largely blank.

I turn to the cover page. It's Chelsea's diary.

K. F. FLEMING

CHAPTER NINETEEN

Diary of Chelsea Green 2020

Chelsea's diary is written in a childish scrawl, a new page for each entry, which is dated and very brief. It's almost as if it was done in haste. I glance at the first recording. It's interesting that Chelsea didn't start her diary until after she moved into Oak Tree Lodge. Did she not have a life before, I'm wondering. What was she doing through December, for example? Where was she living? I don't remember ever asking her about her past, and she certainly never talked about it.

I turn to the first page.

Saturday, Jan 18th, I've been here at Oak Tree Lodge for a week now. It's a good vibe. My room is nice and sunny, and it has a fireplace. Doesn't go, but dreamy to look at. I'm having a blast with my new job and a great boss.

I like the people at the restaurant, and they all seem to like me.

Good, good to know, I'm thinking. Chelsea liked it here. That figures. She should be happy. She got the best room at Oak Tree Lodge. Frank was annoyed. He wanted to move across the hallway into that room when it became vacant. There was no way I was going to let that happen. I turn the page. She's jumped two weeks. Not much of a writer, then.

Sunday, Feb 2nd, I forgot to say how happy Prince is. I thought he might find it hard to settle into a new place, especially somewhere in the city, but he's loving it here. There's a garden and a cat-door so he can go in and out. Everyone strokes him and makes a fuss of him, even Leo, although sometimes he gets a bit precious when Prince sharpens his claws on the rugs and leaves fur on the dining room chairs.

Thank you, Leo, thank you very much for letting me bring my cat with me into your beautiful home and not worrying when he destroys the furnishings. Why is there so much ingratitude in the world?

Friday, Feb 14th, Valentine's Day. Very busy at the restaurant. Boss paid me overtime for working late (just as well). Q sent me roses. Said we'd go out tomorrow night to make up. Roz is very friendly and reminds me of my mum. Looks out for Frank all the time. There's something going on there. Not quite sure what, but definitely something. Roz needs to smoke less, but at least she goes outside to light up. Leo is very particular about this.

I remember Chelsea's roses. She put them on the dining room table. Roz told her it was very generous to share them like that. And it was. I recall thinking what a sweet girl she was. Sexy too.

Sunday, Feb 16th, I don't know what to make of Julius. He has a girlfriend, who bosses him around, but he's serious and smart and normal. Wish I could say the same about the others. Frank skulks in his room, and Leo reminds me of someone.

I'm wondering who my look-alike is as I turn the page.

Thursday, Feb 20th, Submitted my résumé today, fingers crossed ☺. Frank is a lot more friendly today. I made him laugh. I feel sorry for him. He needs a wheelchair sometimes.

I sometimes wonder about Frank and his wheelchair. Some days he spends hours in it, especially in the evenings, but then he's perfectly capable of walking on his own two feet out the door and being away for hours.

Saturday, Feb 22nd, Leo is up himself, and a bit creepy, but okay, overall. Doesn't have a girlfriend (no wonder). Not like Julius. Still haven't heard about part (sob).

Me, creepy? I remember that day I asked Chelsea if she knew her bra was showing. There's no helping some people. Jesus, pardon me, Chelsea. Next time, I'll just let you go about looking all slutty.

Saturday, Feb 28th, I really need to go on a diet in case I get the part. Still haven't heard. Need a different job. Too many late nights, drinking too much.

Good idea, Chelsea, and while we're on that, maybe you should write your diary before you start drinking because you are making up a whole lot of crap.

Monday, March 2nd, Frank came to the restaurant last night. BIG TIP. I misjudged him. He's really a lovely man.

Was he in his wheelchair, I'm asking myself.

Sunday, March 8th, A bit late with rent. Drinking too much again. Didn't get part. Leo is an arsehole. One minute he's cool, and then he's a prize prick, all lechy. I won't tell Q. He's got a temper, and I do need somewhere to live.

You got that right, Chelsea, about Quentin's temper, I mean.

Tuesday, March 10th, I really need to find a new place. I want somewhere close. I love it around here and have lots of friends. I love everyone except a certain person. I've got to get away from him. He's beyond weird. Q is coming to take me out soon. Yay! Will wear my denim dress.

I turn the pages for more. There's nothing. Chelsea Green's diary ended on Tuesday, March 10th.

I have just two questions.

How come you've got the diary, Meg? Where did you find it? I was very careful when I cleaned out Chelsea's room, maybe not as thorough as Edith, but I'm pretty sure I would have seen Chelsea's diary unless she had it hidden somewhere really safe. Like up the chimney or wherever, in which case how did you find it? How could you have possibly found it? It's not as if you just fell over it or came across it as you were climbing into bed or opening a window. You must have been searching for it. But why? How did you even guess that it might exist?

And my second question is, why are you showing it to Julius and not to me? This is not very couplish. It makes me feel excluded. Why are you even talking to that troll?

I suppose, when I think about it, I've got a third question. This is for Chelsea. Who is the certain weird person in your diary? I would really like to know the answer to this question.

Chelsea, I'm really sick of you. I've had enough of you. You're no longer here. The rent is no longer coming in. You're gone. You're nowhere.

But sometimes I think you're still here because you're taking up space; you're living rent-free in my head.

K. F. FLEMING

CHAPTER TWENTY

SATURDAY 4th APRIL

We're half-way through week-two of lockdown. It seems like a lifetime.

Jokes are doing the rounds: witty things like *We ran out of toilet paper today, so now we're using lettuce leaves. And that was just the tip of the iceberg.*

Roz doesn't find this joke the least bit funny. She says it's gallows-humour, and there is a time and a place. And, of course, she's very into lettuce. It's her staple. That's when she's not munching a carrot.

She is keeping the whiteboard updated. Under CASES, she has written 950. Because she wants to make sure we can track progress, she has written (82 new cases) next to 950. She thinks we can't remember that there were 868 cases yesterday and can't add 82. She spends a lot of time in the kitchen, clutching her cupid-and-hearts coffee cup and staring at the whiteboard.

Tempers are frayed.

Mainly mine. Meg. It's always Meg. I've not made as much progress with her as I would like. One minute, she's chatty and attentive, and then she gets that remote look in her eyes as if she's missing London. I guess it must be hard for her, being away from home, especially when there are just as many cases in London, more, in fact. I think she's as scared as everyone else. Boris Johnson, the Prime Minister of Britain, has tested positive for the coronavirus, and he's having a baby.

Meg seems very upset about this. She keeps saying how tough it must be for his wife, not knowing if her unborn child will ever have a father. I guess that would be tough, but there will never be any shortage of money, will there, you know, for nannies and baby clothes? And a new line of would-be daddies will be forming an orderly queue in no time at all.

Things were definitely better with Julius in quarantine. Roz took charge of his meals, delivering them to his door on disposable plates and cups. She also monitored his bathroom visits. I asked her how she was going to look after that. She said she had read up on it and that, as long as Julius confined his business to the toilet area and went without a shower, she could manage. She said she would do a deep clean each time. She also suggested that if I made my bathroom area available, it would be helpful and that I would be doing my bit.

I pretended I didn't hear this, because there was no way I was having all and sundry of Oak Tree Lodge marauding upstairs, poking about and pretending to be above their station. This is exactly what I have to guard against.

With Julius, it turned out to be a false-alarm. The results were sent through by text the next day on his cell-phone. Negative. Pity really. The dynamics of Oak Tree Lodge changed completely with Julius off the scene. I had a clear run at things, and, I have to admit, I come into my own when I don't have to worry about competition. It's not that I think Julius has a chance with Meg (she clearly despises him); it's just that he's always in the way. I note that he's always strutting his stuff like he's got something to strut. He really is a weed, with spindly legs that make me think of chickens. But it puts me off my stride. It reminds me of what Princess Diana said about there being *three people in this marriage*.

I regret that business with Quentin and the cat: fortunately, Meg was not privy to the whole sorry incident, but Roz has clearly filled her in because I've noticed a change in Meg since then. She's watching me a lot. This could be my imagination. She could be just, you know, checking out the goods. Guys do this a lot. But so do girls. They're worse, if anything, always wanting a perfect profile and lots of hair and a Daniel Craig body. On top of that, they want to know how you handle yourself and how chill you are in every situation. They really are relentless.

I haven't asked Meg about the man in the car or Chelsea's diary. Not yet. I'm biding my time—mainly because I don't know how to broach it. I don't want to come across as checking on her. It's very difficult to defend spying on people. Girls have that way of turning it back on you. I watched a documentary once where the husband confronted his wife with infidelity, and he had to apologise for invading her privacy or else *she would never speak to him again*. Imagine that: everything is on the table and perfectly okay apart from being caught out. Wow! *Officer, yes, I did plan to put that bomb there, but how dare you put me under surveillance. What about my privacy?*

So it's not that easy. In fact, it's a minefield. I'm hoping the right time will present itself, and I can just say something casual like, *did you have fun the other day, you know when you went out with that guy that you don't mention?*

Maybe I won't put it quite like that.

But there's other stuff on my mind as well. The house is a mess, and I am missing Edith, my cleaning lady. She was great in the kitchen, taking a scouring pad to the hob and oven when necessary and even getting down on her knees to wash the floor. Timber floors are lovely in an old home but not very practical in a kitchen. The boards are tongue-and-groove and closely fitted, but, over the years, gaps have appeared between some of them. So crumbs and bits get trapped. Edith was conscientious about this part of the house and sometimes used a toothbrush to flick out particles of food.

And she was very good at polishing. The brass knocker on the front door gleamed. And there is an old Windsor brass letter plate, which she lavished her attention on. She had to stand outside to carry out these tasks. In the sunshine. She turned it into an outing because she could chat with the passers-by.

Dusting wasn't her strong point. The dresser in the kitchen had a sheen to it, a burnish. Edith oiled it and then buffed it. Not every week, but more often than needed, in my opinion. And in the meantime, cobwebs quivered under beds and in corners. She had a little trick of shifting things about. The couch would be moved out from the wall a little, and the hall runner would be left askew. Of course, the subtext was, I've cleaned this area, in case you're wondering. See, I've moved the furniture to get at every corner. But, of course, she hadn't. I would check.

I used to worry about these omissions. But now I'm thinking Edith did a pretty good job.

Frank is the only person in our little bubble who is completely upbeat, as if the virus is a blessing. He's been playing the piano all morning. "As Time Goes By", as usual. It's never anything else. I suppose it's the perfect song when you're in lockdown, counting the hours and the days. Just for the record, it's day ten of lockdown, with eighteen days to go, which is four hundred and thirty-two hours.

That's good as far as I'm concerned. It's a lifetime, a lifetime, for Meg and me to get to know each other. I'm planning another dinner. I'll be better prepared this time. The candles were a great idea, but I think I'll try some different music. I notice Meg plays a lot of Ed Sheeran and Adele in her room. I plan to download a playlist from Spotify; that's when I work out how to do this. I realise now that I was rushing things. Girls like a guy to take the lead, but taking the lead is tricky. It has to be carefully calibrated: not too weak but not too strong, either. It's like a dance, a waltz. You have to offer a firm hand, but your touch must be light. And then, of course, the biggest issue, the elephant in the room, is when to make your move. There's that rule enshrined in every girl's sex dossier: *don't do it on the first date. Don't be a slut.* Poor Meg. She must be so confused about how to get it right.

Frank has finished playing the piano (thank God) and is in the kitchen reading what looks like a document, something typed up with headings and paragraphing and spacing. I ask him what it is. The whole time Frank has been at Oak Tree, I've never seen him read anything. He watches television a lot, mainly golf. He is genuinely fascinated by the stroke of the club and the trajectory of the tiny white ball. He leans forward in his chair when the flag is lifted on the green and grunts with pleasure when the ball is putted into the hole. And I note he often touches himself at precisely this point. I try not to look, but I know that Roz has noticed it too. It's always an eyebrows-to-hairline moment.

'What's that, mate?' I ask. 'Looks official.' Frank is wearing that floral shirt of his. I guess his woollen number must have become too much, even for him.

'It's a will,' he says without looking up.

'You're not sick, are you?' asks Roz. 'You haven't, you know, got what Julius had?'

'Roz, Julius tested negative; you know that,' I say.

'It's my mum's will,' says Frank.

'I didn't know you had a mum,' I say.

'I don't,' says Frank, 'not anymore.'

'Jesus, Frank,' I say. 'I'm so sorry.'

'She's been in hospital. Heart disease. It was time.' Frank turns the page of the document. I'm wondering why he is reading this very private document in front of everyone. Why isn't he sequestered in his room for this sacred moment?

'Did she leave you everything?' asks Roz.

Roz is socially challenged. I think I've mentioned this before. What sort of a question is this? What is she thinking?

'Will there be a funeral?' I ask.

'As a matter of fact, she did,' says Frank, looking up at Roz with a grin.

'It must be a good feeling to know you've come into money,' says Roz.

'Are you going to the funeral?' I ask. What is wrong with Roz?

'It is,' says Frank. Am I invisible? Frank is definitely far more focused on his windfall than any send-off for his mum.

'I guess it will be difficult to hold a funeral under level four,' I persist.

'Mum was in Wellington. I can't get there. I've issued instructions as the next of kin.'

'Well done. Must be hard to know what to do,' I say.

Frank turns to the next page. This is some will, I'm thinking: a lot of stuff to disburse. Frank's mum might have been one of those penny-pinching dowagers who lived in penury while their fortune built up exponentially in a bank or lawyer's trust account.

'There's not much precedent to go by. Everything's got so weird,' I persevere.

'She'll be cremated and then scattered,' says Frank.

'Where? Did she have a favourite, go-to place?' asks Roz. She's looking out the kitchen window as she says this as if she's wondering if her herb garden or compost might be the perfect resting place.

I don't think Frank knows the answer to this. He finishes reading the will and folds it up. And now he's springing up and taking himself off to his room. He's humming as he goes. And then that piece again. Frank is playing it allegro. It's jaunty and fast. I don't believe this is how it sounded in "Casablanca". Rick was always sad and introspective. And dignified. I close the door between the kitchen and hallway.

I couldn't help noticing that Frank has made an effort with his appearance. It looks as though he's recently spent some time in the bathroom. His hair is okay for once, and he is freshly shaved. Maybe he's togged up for his mother. He can't be at her funeral, but he can smarten himself up, you know, stand to attention in absentia, as old soldiers do on ANZAC day.

And the floral shirt must be a kind of tribute, although, I must say, if he wanted to honour his mother, he should have just washed his checked shirt. I don't think a floral shirt is very respectful. It speaks to celebration and fun and, quite frankly, a fuck-you-what-took-you-so-long attitude. There's a referendum on assisted dying in November. Frank will be rooting for that, I'm picking.

Quentin was right about one thing around here. It really is a nuthouse. It's been four days since his visit. I guess he didn't go to the police after all. He must have calmed down. He certainly needed to.

CHAPTER TWENTY-ONE

SUNDAY 5th APRIL

There's been another murder.

It wasn't in the arcade this time. It was in the city graveyard. The graveyard is quite close to here, at the end of the road at the T-junction. That's where the body was discovered, under the bridge by a walker out with his dog. It was inevitable. There's nothing else to do these days except go for a walk. And even that is severely limited. Too bad if you're dreaming about being by the sea or taking your boat out for a fish. It's a bitch: you don't have to go to work, but time off is more like being in a correctional facility than on holiday.

Julius is the one to announce the discovery of this latest development. He's glued to the internet, checking out the latest breaking news minute by minute. So he's always got the heads up. I guess it's the next best thing to getting the scoop, which he is forever sleuthing out, to no avail.

He's waited until everyone happens to be in the kitchen. It's mid-morning, and Roz is brewing coffee. Meg looks as though she's been out for a run. She is flushed and dressed in a tee-shirt, trainers and pink silk shorts. She really has very nice legs, toned and muscled, but also slender. I think I may have already mentioned this: I'm a leg man, amongst other things. Her hair is tied back in a high ponytail, and it's a bit matted around her temples: not her best look. She needs a stylist to tell her these things. Even Frank has put in an appearance. He's brought his laundry basket with him. There doesn't seem to be much in it, just that floral shirt that he had on yesterday.

For once Julius is dressed properly, as if he's about to put in a report or interview someone. He's got his jeans on and a white cotton shirt. I suppose this is his idea of what a journalist on the job would look like. It's a relief not to have to look at his chest.

'Listen up,' says Julius. 'This is on the *Herald* site this morning.' He is standing by the sideboard, staring at his phone. And then he looks up at us and pulls the open collar of his shirt forward as if it's too tight for him (when actually he's swimming in it) before reading from his screen: '*A body has been found this morning in an inner-city graveyard.*' Julius pauses for effect and looks up again at our little domestic gathering. Roz gasps and turns away from her coffee machine. She takes a seat at the dining room table and pushes up the sleeves of her blouse. Frank has put down his laundry basket but remains standing. Meg has retreated to the edge of the room by the door to the hallway. I sit down next to Roz. Julius is making a complete spectacle of himself. He needs to get a grip.

He waits until we're all settled. '*Emergency services were called after a body was found partially buried beside a derelict monument in a remote part of the cemetery,*' he continues. '*Police have confirmed officers and emergency staff were called to the scene around 5.00 am.*

'*It is believed the body was discovered by a man out for an early morning walk with his dog. A formal identification process has yet to be undertaken.*' Julius pauses as he takes this in. It's as if he's reading it for the first time.

'*A spokeswoman said police are now making a number of enquiries into the circumstances of the death.*

'*No further information is available at the moment.*'

Julius shuts off his phone and eyeballs each of us in turn.

'Christ, it's like we're living inside an Agatha Christie novel,' says Roz. 'First, Janet Lane, now this.' She's fumbling for her cigarettes and then thinks better of it.

'And Chelsea,' says Meg.

'What about Chelsea?' asks Frank.

'She's gone too,' says Meg. 'That's three. Three young girls.'

'We don't know if it's a girl,' I say.

'There's only one inner-city cemetery,' says Julius, 'and that's the one down the road. Way too close for comfort.'

Roz jerks her head up at Julius and narrows her eyes so tightly that there's not much left, just slits and black mascara.

'There's a pattern,' says Julius, nodding to himself with all the authority of a third-rate detective.

'You can't possibly conclude that,' I say. 'We don't know who the victim is. It could be one of the homeless people from around here or someone who was out for a stroll and had a heart attack, or someone who slipped and fell. The paths in the cemetery are uneven and broken in places.'

I let that hang in the air, and then I say what I really want to say. To Meg. 'And we don't know what happened to Chelsea.' I turn to look at her. She's become very interested in Chelsea all of a sudden. And she's been secretive. She's found Chelsea's diary somehow and read it, no, *studied* it. And she hasn't mentioned it to me. I really do need to have things out with her.

And, as I'm looking at her, she pulls her hair out of her ponytail and plumps it up and flicks it back. It is an elaborate movement, almost a dance. It reminds me of flamingos on the flirt. I'm thinking all is forgiven. Meg, I know how things are. All you want to do is chill and be a tourist and have intelligent, cool people around you and live in a place with lovely Edwardian architecture and have a handsome guy to look after you. Well, you came to the right place. I am your destiny. I will make everything all right. These dead girls, you are not them. You will be okay. I'll make sure of that. You just have to trust me and be nice to me.

Roz has her arms outstretched on the table, in that way of criminals under interrogation who are about to offer something that will change the whole course of the investigation. 'What I don't get,' she says, 'is the stupidity of people. We're supposed to be social distancing. If this is another murder, then we have a serious problem. This guy must be insane, like certifiably. You can't kill someone from a safe social distance. You are endangering people. He needs to think things through a bit more carefully.'

There is nothing to say to this. Even Julius is silent.

'There's nothing remotely rational about murder,' I say finally. 'Normal behaviours don't apply here. I think adhering to the Health Ministry's guidelines would be the last thing on his or her mind when he's, you know, stoving in someone's head or stabbing them or choking the breath out of them.' I'm aware that I've maybe provided too many examples of how someone can be murdered and take a breath.

'I don't know about that,' says Julius. 'Plenty of perfectly reasonable people have committed murder. Most killers, in fact, are highly intelligent and logical. And calm,' he adds. 'The man next door, who cleans his car once a week and keeps his roses pruned and wouldn't hurt a fly, often turns out to be the serial killer.' Julius is obviously more than satisfied with this forensic take on things because he is looking to Meg for approval. And now he squares his shoulders and rolls them not once, but twice. I think I have more urgent things to do, like checking the mailbox or taking a dump, and I get up to leave.

'Just bear with me,' says Julius, raising his right hand, palm out. 'I think we should all give some thought to our movements last night. It's just a matter of time before the police come knocking again. It will save a lot of trouble and inconvenience if we can all account for ourselves.'

'What has this got to do with you?' I ask.

'Look, mate, the police are coming. It's inevitable. What's wrong with getting our stories straight? I can record everything and maybe just get everyone to sign and hand it over to the police.'

'Makes sense,' says Roz. 'Sort of like an affidavit. We want the police in and out as quickly as possible. We don't want them coming into our bubble. And sometimes it's hard to remember what you had for breakfast, let alone what you did last night.'

'So we're all agreed?' asks Julius.

'Just so long as this isn't going to be part of one of your bullshit assignments,' I say.

Julius grabs his clipboard from the floor and unlatches the pen. 'So who wants to start?' he asks.

'Well, I stayed in all night,' says Roz, folding her arms and leaning back. 'I can't speak for everyone else.'

'Same,' says Meg.

'Same,' I say. I like echoing Meg. It makes us sound like a couple: staying in all night in the same house. Next time it will be in the same room and the same bed, my four-poster. And she will be tied to it.

'Did anyone go out last night?' asks Julius.

'No,' says Frank.

'I definitely heard someone go out,' says Meg. 'I remember because I couldn't get to sleep. I was too hot. I got up to open the front window, and I heard the front door open and close.'

'Are you sure?' I ask. Oh, Meg, I'm thinking, if only I'd known you couldn't sleep, I would have been there for you. I would have given you something to help you sleep. Like a baby. Like a babe, baby.

'I'm positive,' says Meg. 'And I thought I heard a male voice.'

'Whose?' asks Julius.

'Hard to say; it was more a throat-clearing than a voice.'

Of course, we all know that Frank is always honking and grunting. He feels the gaze of everyone upon him.

'For fuck's sake,' says Frank. 'So now I'm the bloody Graveyard Ripper.' Frank is looking to Roz, who is managing to acknowledge him and look away at the same time.

'I didn't hear anything,' she says. 'And I'm a light sleeper. A fly or a bee or even a moth in the house is all it takes. I didn't hear anything. Nothing at all. And I definitely would have noticed if anyone went out in the middle of the night.'

'Right, that's that then,' says Frank, 'and unless anyone has any objection, I'll be getting on with my washing.' He reaches down and picks up his laundry basket.

But Julius doesn't seem satisfied. He's not finished with Frank. He wants a cross-examination of some sort but doesn't know how to keep Frank in the room. He's casting around for inspiration, which finally comes to him. 'It's Roz's day for laundry,' he says. 'Everyone knows that.'

'Jesus, it's like the bloody Gestapo around here,' says Frank. 'Worse, at least you knew where you were with them.'

'It's okay,' says Roz. 'Frank is welcome to put his stuff in with mine. I haven't got much.'

This is a first. Roz is rigid about the laundry roster. And she is fastidious about her own washing, especially her undergarments. The prospect of having Frank's stuff in with hers is usually grounds for a full-on melt down.

'Here,' says Frank, handing Roz the basket, and with that, he retreats down the hallway and away from Julius's courtroom.

But here is the news of the day, the event that has eclipsed everything on the social calendar so far: Meg has asked me out on a date. How about that? I can't believe it. She wants us to spend time together away from everyone else. She seems to have got over the Quentin incident with Prince. She has suggested a walk.

At dusk in the graveyard.

So romantic. I can't wait.

CHAPTER TWENTY-TWO

SUNDAY 5th APRIL CONTINUED

This date-night invitation was issued straight after the tedious incident in the kitchen. Julius thought he was so cool, taking charge like that with his clipboard and psychobabble, but my Meg could see right through him. She really is the full package: smart and sexy and switched-on. She gets me. She's been playing hard-to-get. I see that now, stringing Julius along to keep me on my toes.

After Frank takes off, Roz goes out to the laundry, and Julius leaves the house, probably on the hunt for material to pad out his D-grade assignment. Meg is in the garden by this time doing what I can only assume are warm-down exercises. It doesn't look like yoga. She's hoisted her right leg up on the trestle and is leaning over her thigh with her toe pointed towards her. She spends about ten seconds on each side, her torso in a tight bend. Then she gets down on the grass and, folding her legs underneath, stretches her arms forward and brings her head to the ground. Fifteen seconds for this sexy pose of supplication. Is it meant for me? Finally, with her back to me, she bends over and puts her palms on the ground. Meg's shorts are not those modest, mid-calf lycra arrangements that hug the body. They are micro with splits at the sides, so that when she executes this movement, the silk of the garment rides up, and her haunches are on full display.

Her hair is fanning in front of her, and she looks like an angel falling from the sky. She is exactly that, an angel sent to me from heaven.

I don't want to be caught watching, but I'm finding it impossible to look away. I can't help thinking Meg is performing for me because, as soon as she straightens up, she throws her hair back and looks right at me through the kitchen window. Then she parts her lips in a slow smile and extends her arms up over her head, and reaches for the sky. Her top comes up, and I can see her midriff and a hint of red beneath her shorts.

I move away from the window and sit down, pulling the chair under the dining table to conceal the bulge in my pants. I'd like to join her in the garden, take her a glass of water or something so that we can sit together in the open air like we're hanging out al-fresco.

But the moment is lost. Meg skips inside and goes to the sink. She turns on the cold tap and splashes water on her face. She then wipes her hands on her top. That fabric again. Whatever Meg's wearing, it's transparent when wet.

And then those magical words: 'Let's go for a walk. Just you and me, Leo. To the graveyard.' She's doing that Lolita thing with her mouth again, and there's a lot of tongue showing when she says my name. God, I love this girl.

'Sure,' I say. I'd like to get up and move closer to her, but I'm not ready yet, and I don't want to put her off. 'Great idea, an interesting place, so much history.' I wish I hadn't said this last bit. How can graveyards be anything other than full of history? They're full of dead people, for God's sake.

Meg doesn't seem to notice my gaffe.

'It's a date, then,' she says and glides out the door. I can hear her going into the bathroom, and I can feel that throb again, heavy and insistent. Don't do it, Leo, I tell myself. You'll be seeing her soon enough. It'll be the real deal. You and Meg, naked in your bed with all the time in the world.

It's lucky I'm having a good-hair day. I've run out of my chamomile conditioner, and nothing else seems to do the trick. I will have to take a shower, though, and try to find a different shirt.

Speaking of shirts, Roz has come back inside with Frank's. It's obviously been through the cycle (I can see Roz's washing on the line), but she's not satisfied. She's filling the sink with water and she's brandishing a scrubbing brush and squirting detergent on the collar. Since when did Frank earn these ministrations from Roz? I leave her to it and head for my apartment. I need time to get ready.

And now Meg is texting me. *Can we make it 6:00 pm?*

Sure, I text back.

Kinda weird, eh, texting when you're right here in the house?

Kinda, but cute, I text back. I want to add, *like you,* but I resist.

Yeah, it's private, you know. No eavesdroppers. Makes it more like a proper date, like normal people have, you know, who live in different houses on different streets.

☺ I send back. I want to make it a heart instead of a smiley face. But I decide to keep that for next time.

I know exactly what she means. Julius is always in the way, pretending to be on that infernal phone of his, but, actually, listening and weighing and judging. I really would like to suggest he find alternative accommodation, but I suppose, under level four, that might not seem very community spirited. We are being told to shelter in place, stay in our bubble and all that. And *look after each other, be kind*. We're *the team of five million*, we keep being told.

The graveyard is a beautiful place, with paths laid out for strollers. It's better than the park, actually, with lots of old oaks and elms and stonework. And it's not just a walk; it's an insight into how things used to be in the nineteenth century. You realise how short the average lifespan was. Most people didn't make middle age, and childhood was obviously a perilous phase because there are dozens of monuments to tiny children. "One and a half years" is inscribed on the headstone of one family plot. I think about that little toddler from time to time, how his last days were, and how sad his mum and dad must have been.

I visit the graveyard a lot. It's a perfect venue for my first date with Meg. I know so much about this place and can educate Meg. And this will, of course, put my stocks up. Girls like guys who know stuff. This is a perfect opportunity.

Meg has become a different person since the announcement of the latest death this morning. She has become strangely overfamiliar, over-attentive, and even clingy, touching me all the time. Don't get me wrong, I like to be touched, but there's something *off* about it all, as if the behaviour filter, the bit that moderates social interaction, has been scooped out of her brain.

I really should be pleased, but I was more than slightly put off when she came bursting into the kitchen right at 6:00 pm dressed in what I can only describe as full-on date-rape gear.

At first glance, it seems an okay dress for an evening walk in a cemetery. It is black and modestly long, with side slits. But those dresses are the worst. They purport to hide things, but, in fact, everything is on display and right there if you take the time to look. And, of course, that is the whole point. You are forced to look and look and look. The more you look, the more you see: the curve of Meg's voluptuous breasts, the run of her legs from ankle to thigh, and the slope of her torso tapering into a wasp-waist. If I had to sum up the dress in two words, I'd say *red carpet*. Just think Angelina Jolie, standing next to Brad Pitt. So she brought this all the way from London to little old New Zealand. And now she's put it on for me to walk in a public place. What I would really like to do is take her straight up to my bedroom and take it off. She's even wearing heels of some kind.

I immediately sit down. I haven't put my boots on because, although they give me an extra inch, they're too tight to walk any distance. I'll need to change before we go out unless I can persuade her to put on some flats. Meg comes and sits next to me and folds one leg over the other.

'Well, hello, Leo,' she says in that way of hers and strokes my arm.

'Shh,' says Roz. The news is about to start. And now Julius and Frank have assembled, and the whole of Oak Tree Lodge is turned to the television set.

The murder is the opening item. There's Covid-19 all around, but the news channel is focusing on the body in the cemetery. The dead girl has been identified. Her name is Molly Bell. She worked at Lollipops. She was twenty-four years old and left behind a two-year-old girl. The newsreader is very business-like. And now she has moved on to the number of new Covid cases.

'Maybe Quentin had a point,' says Roz.

'What?' says Julius.

'Things are getting very odd around here. That's the third girl, who has either gone missing or been unaccounted for.'

'Are you counting Chelsea?' asks Julius.

'Yes,' says Roz. 'She's become just another statistic. What do you think, Frank?' She turns to Frank, who snaps his head up at her.

'How the hell should I know?' he says. 'Why are you asking me?'

'Keep your hair on,' she says.

I don't think Frank appreciates this. Trying to keep his hair on is pretty much what he is doing every minute of every day. I've had enough of this merry and stimulating gathering, and stand up.

'I'll just be a minute,' I say to Meg, touching her lightly on the arm. She smiles up at me.

I race up the stairs and change my socks (thinner and silkier) and pull on my boots. I can hear the clip of Meg's shoes along the hallway. I hope those heels are not denting the wooden floor.

And now we're walking out the front door. It's a perfect evening, warm with the sun about to set. Meg links her arm through mine, and I feel a tingle. Her flesh is warm and smooth and taut. She has a spring in her step, in spite of her heels, and really seems in quite a hurry. I wanted to take it slowly, but I guess with everything closed, there's not much to look at. Most of the shop fronts are bare. We pass a kebab place, a wine bar, a second-hand clothing shop and a $2.00 shop. And then we are at the arcade. Meg stops and looks down through the entrance, which leads into the park. I stop with her. She has a sad expression on her face and is looking hard at me.

'Come on,' I say and guide her along the street. I'm wondering if she is up for the cemetery walk and why she suggested it in the first place. And now we're crossing the main road and looking at the entrance with its old stone steps. Meg hitches up her dress a little and leans into me as we walk down. There's an immediate drop in temperature, and she shivers a little.

'What I'd really like to do, Leo, is go to the scene of the crime,' says Meg. 'You know where the girl was killed. I know it sounds macabre, but I've always been fascinated by crime, what motivates people, you know, what drives people to kill. I watch that *Born to Kill* series a lot. I often wonder if people are born evil, or do they become like that?'

I think Meg has spent too much time talking to Julius. And this is not a very romantic date. I really wanted it to be a picnicky kind of gig, like a walk in a park where you admire the flowers and trees and shrubbery. And then kiss behind a tree and admire the sky.

'Hey, fun fact,' I say. 'Did you know people were buried here according to their religion? Anglicans, Catholics, Jews, they've all got their own sections. And Presbyterians and Wesleyans.'

'Is this the way?' asks Meg.

'Yes, she died under the bridge,' I say.

We're passing a huge stone slab with a central monument, the shape of a tower. There's an angel on either side, a sort of Gabriel with monstrous, outstretched wings. The iron railing is rusted and bent. Weeds are growing up through the cracks in the stone.

Meg stops to read the inscription. A boy, aged three, lies here alongside his parents.

A small dog scampers up to the railing and immediately hunkers down to do his business, legs, akimbo, and tail, ramrod perpendicular, as he shudders with the effort of delivery.

'They worshipped separately in life, and I guess death didn't change a thing. There are a lot of very important people buried here: famous politicians of old. William Hobson, for instance, our first Governor General,' I say, trying to ignore the dog and impress Meg. Things are not going well. There's no sun, and the trees are so ancient and thick and tall that they make everything dark and cold.

'Which way now?' asks Meg, turning to me.

'Not far,' I say, moving her away from the sad mausoleum.

'How do you know the way?' asks Meg. She's looking intently at me as she asks this question.

'I come here a lot. It's peaceful. It reminds me of my mum and dad,' I say, hoping for sympathy. Girls like to see your soft side. You have to be human and vulnerable while at the same time being masculine and in charge. It's a tricky navigation.

And then we see it, the final resting place of the girl. It's a little hollow under the bridge, quite dark and damp looking. It has been cordoned off, and there are people milling about, lighting candles and incense and laying flowers. Meg has fallen silent, and I can feel her watching me as we make our way to the group of mourners.

And the dog has reappeared. He's sliding his not-very-private privates along the tussocky grass and seems to be daring us to shoo him away.

Dogs, they're messy things. Give me a cat any day. They somehow manage to shit in the dark and then cover it up.

A bit like The Graveyard Ripper.

CHAPTER TWENTY-THREE

MONDAY 6th APRIL

The visit to the cemetery did not end well. You never want your date to burst into tears when you're just getting warmed up. I'm not sure what triggered it, but Meg was there and then not there.

We were standing together holding hands, and then she shivered. I put my arm around her to keep her warm. I am not sure if she liked this. It seemed to make her shiver even more. I wanted to fold her into me and wrap her up, but I didn't think it would be appropriate with everyone making tributes to a dead girl, a young mother. It would have come across as coarse and insensitive. So I just stood there with her.

And then someone came up and put her arms around both of us and held us for a long moment. She was a total stranger, young, dressed in jeans and a tight top. And then she stepped back and said, 'You've lost someone too.'

'What?' I said. I couldn't think what she was talking about.

'Chelsea, you've lost Chelsea. She's gone. You must miss her. We miss her too.'

I didn't know what to say to this, so I didn't say anything. I certainly wasn't going to mention that she should be socially distancing. I didn't think that would have gone down too well. Meg kept looking at me as if she expected something from me. And then she reached down, took off her shoes and ran from the cemetery.

This was right after I said something about where the body was found. I said something along the lines of, 'A cemetery seems the perfect place to leave a body. Although not that convenient.' And then I think I added, 'It's not as if you can legally bury anyone here. That all stopped over a hundred years ago.' I don't think this was well-received. I was just trying to be informative, you know, like a guide, providing another fun fact for Meg, to entertain her and impress her.

I guess I failed in that. I mean, I don't think I struck the right note.

I suppose it's tough for Meg. Here she is in a strange country, where she had planned all sorts of adventures, touring, sightseeing, and meeting lots of interesting people, and she's stuck inside with the stink of Frank and the tedium of Julius and the latest casualties of Covid-19 filling the news cycle. And on top of all of this, The Graveyard Ripper seems to be on everyone's lips.

The police are making no bones about it if you'll excuse the pun. It's now front page of the newspaper: the dead girl is Molly Bell, aged twenty-four, a mother who worked at Lollipops. There's a pattern with the victims, although the report stops short of saying exactly what it is. There was a sum of money found on Miss Bell, undisclosed by the media, except to say it was substantial. For the first time, there is a hint that Lollipops is a front for a sex parlour.

And then there was an item on the morning TV news. A friend of Molly's was interviewed. She was asked about the money. She couldn't have been more than twenty-four herself and was holding a baby on her lap and looking up. The interviewer was observing safety protocols (she was standing six feet away) while she asked her prying questions, and the cameraman panned the tiny bed-sitter with its neatly made double-bed and cluttered kitchen bench.

'How long have you known Molly?' the interviewer is asking. She is very commanding in her navy blouse and black skirt, and black specs. Doesn't she know how much better she would look if she bothered to get contacts? Glasses are not very feminine. And they're definitely not sexy.

'It must be five years now. I knew her before she came to Lollipops,' answers Molly's friend. Her baby is wriggling and reaching up to her. It's hard to tell if it's a boy or a girl, but it's chubby and new, and I get the feeling it just wants everyone to go away so it can have a cuddle and a feed. The girl rearranges it on her lap.

'How would you describe Molly?' the interviewer asks.

'Molly was an awesome friend,' says the girl. 'She was an awesome person,' she adds.

The interviewer keeps the microphone tilted towards the girl. She definitely needs more from her.

The girl obliges. 'She always put everyone else first.' She pauses and wipes the tears away from one eye and then the other carefully, so as not to ruin her makeup. 'And there was nothing she wouldn't do for her little girl. That wee mite was her sun and moon. Literally. She was her everything.'

'Did Molly have lots of friends?' asks the interviewer.

'Everyone loved Molly. There was something special about her, you know. And people could see that.

You couldn't help but see that. Everyone wanted to be her friend. And she would reach out to people.'

'You mean she would help people?'

'Yes, even though she didn't have very much herself. People around here are struggling too, and she cared, you know. Most people don't care. Well, Molly wasn't like that. Molly would just go right up to someone and give them five dollars or whatever, even though she didn't really have it to spare.'

'But she did have money, didn't she?'

'Well, yes, she had a job, a decent job, and she worked hard.' The girl flashes defiant eyes at the interviewer.

'But you do know she was found with a great deal of cash on her.'

'I don't know anything about that,' says the girl. She is stroking the head of her baby and looking down.

The interviewer, who is hawk-eyed and thin-lipped, reminds me of Julius, except that she is tall and thin, and Julius could easily play Bilbo Baggins in *Lord of The Rings*. She wants the scoop. Never mind about the tragedy of a little girl who has lost her mum and someone who has lost her best friend. This is not enough for the ravenous TV audience, who are at home on the edge of their seats. The girl has sidestepped the question about money. The interviewer needs this answered. Later she will say she was only doing her job.

She flicks the microphone back to herself. 'But what about the money?' she asks again. 'Isn't it a little unusual that she should be carrying so much cash when, you know, she was so poor?'

The girl has clasped her hands together, and now she is lifting her baby up and holding her close and rubbing her back.

'Molly was struggling. We all were. She had a baby girl at home and her mum to support. She needed her tips, you know, at Lollipops. The extras were what got her through each week, you know, helped her to make ends meet. She had rent to pay and doctors' bills for her mum.' The girl is crying again, but her hands are full with her baby, and fat tears gather and run down her cheeks. The cameraman is right there with her, making sure her full story is recorded. In the public interest.

And, *Gotcha*, the interviewer must be thinking because the interview is terminated. She hasn't made a single accusation, but it is there for everyone to see, the invisible subtitle: *Molly Bell was a sex worker.*

'This virus has a lot to answer for,' says Roz. It's the hottest day of the year with record high temperatures predicted, and Roz has rolled up the sleeves of her blouse as far as her elbows. 'I mean, apart from the obvious.'

'Which is?' asks Julius. Julius is standing by the sideboard in a tourniquet-tight, muscle-tee with its usual bullshit logo. Today it reads, *Man plans, God laughs.* So now Julius is quoting from the Bible, as if he's read it. I guarantee he wouldn't even know that there are two parts to that holy book. There ought to be a law against quoting from something you haven't read.

'These poor girls, they're taken advantage of. Just because they're young and pretty, men think they're up for it,' says Roz.

'Well, they are up for it, obviously,' says Julius. 'It's the way of the world.' Julius has moved closer to the TV set and is standing in that macho way of short guys with his legs so wide apart you could step through. He somehow thinks that this spread gives him more height.

'It's one thing to be on the game because you're just plain greedy, but Molly wasn't like that, was she? She had a little girl. And a mother. She had a mother,' says Roz.

'Most people do,' says Julius.

That's exactly the sort of insensitive, offensive crap I expect from Julius, which is precisely why he will never make it as a journalist. News involves people, Julius, in case you haven't noticed. To get the story, you have to be *in tune* with things. I feel so sorry for Poppy. Maybe I'll give her a call sometime, so she can experience what it's like to be with someone intelligent and normal. Someone who knows how to make people feel comfortable.

It's hot enough in here without a full-blown screaming match between Roz and Julius. I take myself upstairs and open my bedroom window. I need to clear my head and plan my next move with Meg.

There's a pattern forming, which I don't like. Meg is all come-on and up-for-it (sorry, Roz) and then she runs out on me. I'm tired of making excuses for her. Either she wants it, or she doesn't. She needs to make up her mind. Piss or get off the pot, isn't that the saying? You've set the table, Meg. Well and truly, laid it out with gleaming cutlery and bone china, ready for the feast. You need to sit there, sit up at the table, ready to eat. And be eaten. A cock-tease. There, I've said it. You're a cock-tease, Meg. And that's never a good thing. Cock-teasers get their comeuppance in the end. They come to a sticky end. I wouldn't want that for you, Meg. You're far too gorgeous. No-one should hurt you. You shouldn't end up like Molly Bell or Janet Lane.

You're too classy and precious. Especially to me. You were made for me. We are meant to be together. I wouldn't want to see you all dirty and dead and discarded under a bridge in the cold, dank dark. You don't deserve this.

I need to lie down and relax. I also need a diazepam. On the way home last night, I visited the twenty-four-hour pharmacy at the end of the street. There was a long queue outside, and I had to wait. There was also a sign asking if you had a temperature or a sore throat. If so, you would not be allowed in. Too bad if you just needed a throat gargle or some paracetamol for a headache. In that case, you had to phone your doctor for guidance. But it's okay if you have a full-blown nervous collapse. Come in, come in, Mr Mad; how can we make you welcome even though you're in the mood to shoot up the whole place?

So I got my diazepam. It was a repeat prescription, no doctor consult required.

I took one last night on the way home, forcing it down with my own saliva. It did the trick. It stopped me from banging on Meg's door and dragging her out and demanding an explanation, and much more besides.

But the effects have worn off, and I need another to get through the day. I pop the blue pill from its tinfoil and swallow it down. I'm by my bedroom window looking down as I do this. It must be a magic pill because Meg has materialised in the garden. She's come out of her lair and is in her two-piece again. It's a different colour: red. The colour of whores. Is that what you are, Meg? An I've-got-my-price kind of girl? If so, I can pay. I'll pay anything. Let's just hope the price is not too high for you. You're walking around (strutting, more like), and you are talking on your phone. You're laughing a lot. *What happened to the tears?*

You're walking over to the shed. And trying the door handle. Why are you doing this? You've already asked me about the shed. And I told you. I told you everything that you needed to know. I didn't mention the hat I stole. It wasn't in the shed at that point. But there are other stolen items. And bits and bobs from previous guests. Chelsea, for instance. She left a lot of stuff behind, apart from underwear and Prince. But that was Chelsea: so careless.

And now the inevitable. Julius has joined her in the garden. She clicks off her phone and tucks it into her bra. Jesus.

'This is like Fort Knox,' I can hear her saying to Julius, with a smile in her voice. I hope she's not doing that Lolita thing again. That would be giving Julius completely the wrong impression.

And then they go around the back of the shed, and I do what I've never done before. I pop a second diazepam.

CHAPTER TWENTY-FOUR

TUESDAY 7th APRIL

Roz has updated the whiteboard. She's taken to doing this right after what has become the most anticipated television event of the day: the Dr Ashley Bloomfield coronavirus bulletin, screened at 1:00 pm, just before *Coronation Street*. With his floppy hair and understated spectacles, our health director is the poster boy for optimism and calm in these times of panic. He stands in his tall, academically lean frame at the podium each day and reads out the grim statistics with Greek stoicism.

He occasionally smiles, just the right amount. He doesn't want to come across as too relaxed, but, at the same time, he wants to instil optimism in the people of New Zealand. We need to know that our sacrifices and discipline are paying off. We're the team of five million. Every statistic is spoken with the utmost reverence as if the person who has tested positive or died is a close relative. We're all one big family. We love one another as if they are our own is the subtext.

Except, we don't. Has Dr Ashley not caught up with what is going on around here, within a one-kilometre radius of Oak Tree Lodge? There's murder and mayhem on the streets. There are two hidden enemies, not one. The team of five million know how to beat the deadly virus, but no-one has a clue what to do about The Graveyard Ripper. Not even the police. They haven't come back to interview us. I'm finding that very strange. Maybe they think they already have their man.

I'm feeling okay after a second diazepam. I don't like to think of myself as drug dependent. That's for old people and sick people. But Meg has been doing my head in. I wonder if she knows this. Does she know that every time she flirts with Julius, Mr Mad starts to take over?

Anyway, I've managed to put myself together and come downstairs. I'm finding it very hot in my jeans and linen shirt, but it's my best look, so I'll stick it out. If Meg wasn't here, I'd probably just wear a tee-shirt and shorts and flip-flops. I settle myself down in the captain's chair (which faces the TV) and prepare to listen. It's not quite a full house: no sign of Frank, but Meg and Roz and Julius are all here. I've decided to play it cool with Meg and act like nothing happened yesterday. I can hardly ask why she was crying yesterday in the cemetery. For one thing, girls don't like to be asked about their emotions. And for another, maybe it should be obvious why Meg broke down and wept. It was all pretty sad when you think about it.

Today there have been fifty-four new cases in our country, bringing the total to 1160. Globally, Dr Bloomfield informs us, there are over a million infections and more than fifty thousand deaths. But this, he says, is the beginning of the flattening of our curve. It's day thirteen, D-Day. And, as predicted, cases are down. This is the first time recoveries have exceeded new cases. He allows himself a smile and looks around at his audience. The Prime Minister is there with him. They make a formidable team. This is leadership at its best. The whole nation from Cape Reinga to Bluff is at home, huddled next to their television sets, hanging on every word. Lives are at stake; livelihoods are on the line. We're the team of five million, pulling together to save one another. And then the end of the news update is heralded by that iconic music from *Coronation Street*. I'd like to watch this. Upstairs in my room. No-one seems to appreciate this insightful program here at Oak Tree. Roz, who takes charge of the remote when Frank is not here, immediately switches off the television. It is as if to watch anything else would be disrespectful to the dead and dying. We must all take a moment of silence to reflect. Fair enough. Except that it's okay for her to glue herself day and night to the E-channel, which is obsessed with everything that can only be described as completely non-E. That is non-essential.

'Boris Johnson has been admitted to hospital,' announces Julius.

Meg is in her red two-piece again, a wrap over it. It's white and delicate-looking. And see-through, so I'm wondering why she has bothered. She's coiled it around herself as if it's a bath towel, and it's tied tightly across her chest so that her breasts are sharply defined and pinkish under the white fabric. She could be wearing nothing. I guess that is the point.

'Oh, how awful,' says Meg. And she unclips her ponytail and shakes her hair loose.

'I wouldn't worry,' says Julius. 'He'll be like, you know, a VIP patient. Nothing will happen to him. He'll be fussed over by a whole team stationed at his bedside, day and night. Not like the poor bastards from the East End or Brixton or wherever.' He's got his muscle-tee on again and seems to have oiled himself up.

Since when did Julius become an expert on the socio-economic groups of London? Since never, that's when. He's at it again: trying to impress Meg.

'How's Poppy?' I ask. 'Have you heard from her lately?'

Julius goes to his default mode whenever he's threatened by me, which is most of the time. He simply pretends I'm invisible and buries himself in his smartphone. Right now he's punching into it and scrolling furiously.

'Listen up,' he says. And then, he pushes his glasses up and looks at each of us, in turn, to make sure we are ready to *listen up*. He clears his throat and somehow manages to flex his biceps without actually moving his arms. Jesus.

'*New Zealand Prime Minister, Jacinda Ardern, has declared the Easter Bunny to be an essential worker in her country, stating that the rabbit can go about its mysterious business this Sunday as usual, despite a nationwide lockdown.*'

'Oh, yeah, it's Easter,' says Roz. 'It's funny how nothing means anything anymore. One day runs into the next. Dates don't matter. Days don't matter. I don't even know what day it is today.'

Roz is just warming up. She has a whole lot more to say, I can tell, but Julius cuts her off. I hope Meg is picking up on this: Julius's complete inability to relate to anything other than his own petty needs.

'*Ardern announced the exception in response to rampant speculation by New Zealand's youngest citizens, who had wondered how the coronavirus crisis might affect the traditional arrival of colourful eggs, chocolates and other treats.*'

'She's a wag,' says Meg. 'You're so lucky to have a leader like her. You know, kind of in charge   but relaxed at the same time.' I love this from Meg. She's obviously aiming this compliment at me. That's exactly how I am: strong but flexible when the need arises, able to read a situation and go with the flow.

'*In a sweeping move,*' continues Julius, '*Ardern also laid to rest any doubts about the Tooth Fairy's status, saying the overnight exchange of gifts for lost teeth will continue.*'

'How cute,' says Meg. 'You really do live in a divine country.'

'*You'll be pleased to know,*' continues Julius, '*that we do consider both the Tooth Fairy and the Easter Bunny to be essential workers.*'

'Wow, Jacinda is lovely. She's got a little girl, hasn't she? Imagine that, being a Prime Minister with a young daughter to look after.' Meg is being very polite to Julius. I hope he appreciates this.

'That was quite a piece, Julius. Who wrote that?' I ask. I'm thinking it's exactly the sort of elegant, funny and factual piece that Julius will never be able to write, except in his fantasies.

'Um, yes, it's from an overseas paper. Chappell, I think.'

'Worth some study,' I suggest, 'you know, to help with your own journalistic style.'

'Here's another editorial. It's headlined, *Don't Be An Egg,*' says Julius. And he's smirking. Yes, he would find that tired old pun amusing.

Roz interrupts him. 'It's so sad,' she says, 'all those children who can't do a real egg hunt. It's not the same, is it, hunting for treasure in your own backyard?'

'Especially if you don't have one,' I say.

'Makes me think of Molly's little girl,' says Roz. 'What kind of Easter is she going to have without her mum?'

And then Meg's phone is ringing. She looks at it as if it is radioactive and then makes for the garden. I can hear it ringing. It's a strange sound, like an old-fashioned land-line buzz, not the musical ringtones of modern devices. She's going behind the shed, and I can still hear the phone. Finally, she must have answered it because I don't hear anything more, not even her voice in the distance.

But I'm hearing something else: it's the ringtone of Meg's phone when she was upstairs with me at her birthday party. It was jaunty and orchestral. And I'm seeing something else. The birthday party phone was red. I remember that quite clearly because it was the same colour as the glorious panties, Meg flashed at me the day she arrived at Oak Tree.

This phone is white.

What I want to know, Meg is why you have two phones.

And while I am thinking about it I realise that the phone Meg took the trouble to bring into the shower was white. And it didn't have a musical ringtone. It was a business-like buzz, that same identical sound that I've just heard here in my kitchen. Who brings a phone into the shower anyway? Red or white? Surely phone calls can wait while you carry out your ablutions. You know, wash and cleanse those parts of yourself that are secret and private.

And now, I'm mentally carrying out a micro-review of the whole bathroom incident. Not only did Meg interrupt her shower to take the call, but she also didn't even finish her shower. I remember thinking how much she needed to clean herself. She must have been all sweaty after sunbathing in the garden with Julius, and yet she simply stepped out, got dressed and left the house.

And there was someone waiting for her outside. This must have been pre-arranged. The phone call was a summons. An urgent summons. There is no other explanation for it. The man in the car was the caller. Who the hell is he, Meg? And what has he got over you? Something important, that's for sure.

I noticed your look of panic when your phone rang. Most people like getting phone calls. Julius, for example, is delighted when someone phones him, which is almost never. It makes him feel validated. How sad is that? But you looked as though it was the call you had been dreading for the whole of your life: the governor of Texas maximum security about to deny the stay of execution, for example. Who has that power over you, Meg? And why does your conversation with him have to be top secret?

Do you have another lover? Is that why I can't get to first base with you? You don't want to be a two-timer? And you don't want to tell me because you think I'll lose interest? Oh, Meg, I would never lose interest. I've never met anyone like you. You're the complete package. You are smart and witty and gorgeous. You're an angel, my angel. You take me to heaven on golden wings. And the best thing is, you *get* me. Not many people do. It takes someone special to appreciate someone with superior qualities. So many people don't take the time to see what is right in front of them.

Take Chelsea, for example. She was too full of herself, making everything about her. She was so busy trying to get to the top of the ladder that she couldn't work out the basics. If she'd just paid more attention to the bottom rung, which she kept falling off, things might have been different.

So, Meg, I have to admit, you've read me well. I'm not the sort to play second fiddle to anyone. I don't do sharing. I don't mind letting people come into my kitchen and garden and use the amenities here at Oak Tree (as long as they are paying up-front), but letting anyone have a piece of my girl is completely off the menu. Whoever this guy is, he needs to understand that. Next time your phone rings, the white one, that is, I might just have to answer it for you, Meg. Maybe the caller and Mr Mad need to get acquainted. There's no time like the present, as the saying goes. I'm thinking I might march out to the shed right now and have it out with whoever the hell is harassing you.

'I'm having a glass of wine,' announces Roz, as she leans into her bar fridge and pulls out a bottle. Alcoholics are secretive about their drinking. They drink alone and hide the empties. Roz thinks that an up-front, brazen announcement somehow puts her in the clear. *Here I am; I'm having a drink in broad daylight for all to see. All legit.* She grabs a tumbler and walks out to the garden. She sets herself up at the trestle and lights up. She's inhaling not just the smoke but the whole cigarette. I'm not all that interested in Roz's addictions, but I can't help noticing the size of the measure she pours herself. I also can't help noticing that she's sculled the contents in one go. I think I'll leave Meg until later. I really don't need a drunken audience when I'm trying to sort things out.

CHAPTER TWENTY-FIVE

WEDNESDAY 8th APRIL

Chelsea Green has finally turned up.

In a manner of speaking. Her body has been found. Not far from here. It was in the park. Not the park exactly. She was found inside the disused public conveniences. They've been closed for some time. The building is very old, turn-of-the-century, last century, that is, and deemed unsafe.

It's an architectural landmark: red brick with herringbone detailing and two oval windows. Imagine that: oval windows in a toilet block. There's even a little sculpture worked into the bricks, depicting a Cupid, complete with quiver and arrows. It really is a beautiful building. And it has been built on the knoll overlooking the city. Whoever built this tiny structure took great pride in his work. Now, the plumbing is rickety, and the porcelain needs replacing. All too expensive to fix. Easier just to close it up and padlock the door, which is exactly what the council did. They created their own problem. It's classified *heritage*: can't be touched. So there it sits, a monument to bygone craftsmanship and current bureaucracy, unfit for purpose and unable to be accessed.

Except by The Graveyard Ripper. At least, that's what the front page of the newspaper is implying. The reporter has really got the scoop this time. The article takes up the whole of the front page and is continued on page two. Eat your heart out, Julius. There are several photographs of Chelsea Green, as well as the toilet block and a statue of Moses and the Tablets.

Julius read the article quietly to himself for once and then left the newspaper on the dining room table. I'm standing behind Roz, who is poring over every detail. I've got my contact lens in, so I can easily read from here. Frank is sitting right next to Roz, and they are reading together. She stops every now and again and lets out a sigh. There is not much detail, but the basics are clear. Chelsea Green has been murdered and is thought to be the third victim of the killer, now widely speculated to be The Graveyard Ripper. I guess *Ripper* means the girls have all been stabbed, although the paper doesn't actually state this.

"Police have been called to the scene of the disused conveniences in Priam Park after a tip-off from a jogger, taking his dog for a run early yesterday," is the opening one-sentence paragraph.

I'm wondering what took the joggers so long. This is a well-worn track. People run around here all the time, summer and winter, day and night.

The article continues: "The building has been cordoned off following the discovery of a body within its precincts.

"A spokesperson for the police said law enforcement was summoned to the scene following an alert put out by a member of the public.

"A witness said that emergency services had to be called to gain entry to the building, which was closed to the public.

"The body, which was of a young girl, recently reported missing in the area, had been in the building for some weeks."

I try not to think about that: Chelsea in those toilets for some weeks. In high summer. I guess the dog picked up on it. It has been extremely hot lately, even for summer.

"'It's the last thing you imagine finding when you're out on a sunny morning for a run with your dog,' said the jogger."

He is described as a twenty-nine-year-old father of two who lives locally.

"'I mean, it's unimaginable. If it hadn't been for my dog, I would have gone right past. Rex is a trained elite rescue dog. He's an Urban Search and Rescue dog, used to trouble and retrieval, although in this case, it was too late, obviously. I tried to pull him away, but he was having none of it.'

"The young man, who doesn't want to be identified, said he was pleased to be instrumental in helping the police solve what was obviously a murder case, but that it was his dog, really, who is the hero. If it hadn't been for Rex refusing to budge, he would never have alerted the police. There were no visible signs of anything strange about the toilet block. The body could have stayed there undiscovered for years.

"'I'm just glad that the girl, whoever she is, has been found and can now be looked after and laid to rest properly.'"

Somehow this news item, which should be about Chelsea, is all about Rex, the dog. Tone-deaf, that's what it is. I'm thinking Julius will fit right in when he finally gets a job as a reporter.

The article says that the death is being treated as suspicious and has been referred to the coroner. And then it goes on to call for any information that the public might have that would help the police with their inquiries. It ends with a spokesperson for the police issuing a warning to the public to stay home and take precautions. The phrase, *serial killer,* is used for the first time.

Isn't that precisely what we're doing, Mr Plod, I'm thinking. Staying home and taking precautions. Keeping away from the coronavirus and anybody who could be carrying it. Sitting inside day after day behind locked doors in our bubbles, going mad with boredom. Washing our hands, rinsing the lettuce and baby spinach leaves one by one. Obviously, it's not working. Quite the opposite, in fact. Empty streets and parks are the perfect venues for a murder. There's no-one to see, no witnesses. The Graveyard Ripper is one smart dude. And Covid-19 is like winning lotto for him. Or her. Why do men always get a bad rap?

'Poor Chelsea,' says Roz. She gets up from the table and pours herself a glass of wine.

That's quite okay, Roz. If this isn't the time for a glass of wine, then what is? And besides, who am I to judge?

Frank says, 'I miss that Chelsea.' Frank is in his usual get-up, checked shirt and corduroy trousers, and he's starting to steam. I open up the kitchen windows. Why doesn't he put his floral shirt on? At least it's summery and clean. I know this because Roz fussed over it, trying to get some stains out. 'She was a good girl. I liked her a lot,' he continues.

Obviously, Frank. We all miss her. What, do you think this makes you a sensitive human being because you miss someone who you lived with and shared meals with and talked with every day? Only a complete monster or serious narcissist wouldn't miss Chelsea. She was here, and then she wasn't here. We all miss her.

'It's just not the same without Chelsea,' says Roz. 'There was something very grounded about her. She was a breath of fresh air.'

Jesus, Roz, I'm thinking. Poor choice of words. I don't think she's *a breath of fresh air* any longer. And *grounded*?

'It was nice having someone young and innocent around the place,' she continues, taking a sip of wine. 'She was such a friendly girl.'

'Too friendly, obviously,' says Julius. 'Look where it got her.'

'I really don't understand it. Who would want to murder a beautiful young girl like that? She never did anyone any harm. She wouldn't hurt a fly. And everyone loved her. She was such a warm person. Not judgemental,' continues Roz.

'I don't know about that,' says Julius.

'What do you mean?' asks Roz. Her eyebrows have shot up, and she is leaning forward in that way of hers when she senses something salacious is about to drop.

'She didn't like everyone. She had problems like everyone else,' says Julius.

'How do you know that?' asks Roz. She has put her wine glass down on the table, and her eyes have grown wide.

'She wrote about it in her diary,' says Julius. He's looking at his phone while he says this as if he's not really at all interested in what is obviously a bombshell.

'I didn't know she had a diary,' says Roz.

'Well, she did. Meg found it in her room and showed it to me.'

'Where did she find it? I mean, how could that have possibly happened? The police came and searched her room, right?' Roz takes another sip of her wine. This is information overload, and she needs time to think.

'And who leaves a diary behind, anyway?' she continues. 'It's kind of personal. I always thought it was weird, Chelsea going off like that without Prince.' She twists her neck around to look at me as if I am responsible for Prince being left behind, as if I kidnapped him or something. I don't say anything.

'Quentin was right. It's unbelievable that she would do that. And her diary as well. Why would she do that?' She directs this question to Julius.

'How should I know?' says Julius.

'So, did you read her diary?'

'I did.'

'Do you think you should have done that? I mean, it's like eavesdropping. Worse, because people write personal stuff in their diaries.'

Julius ignores this.

'What was in it?' asks Roz.

'I'd rather not say. She wrote about people here at Oak Tree Lodge. And it wasn't all complimentary.'

'Did I get a mention?' asks Roz.

'No,' lies Julius.

'What about me?' asks Frank. He has stood up, and I can't help noticing how big he is.

'She said you came to the restaurant one time and left a big tip for her.'

'What made you do that,' asks Roz, 'when you're always crying poor?'

'Why wouldn't I do that?' snaps Frank. 'And, anyway, I'm not so poor. Not anymore. I'll be moving

out of here first chance I get. As soon as we come out of
lockdown.'

The first I've heard of it, I'm thinking. I know
Frank's mum died. She must have left him a
bundle.

'Did you come into a lot of money?' I ask.

'I did. About time.'

And then Roz pipes up, 'I'm going too. I'm
getting my own place. Frank has agreed to lend me
money for a deposit. Haven't you, Frank?'

Frank has a look on his face that says *we'll see
about that*. He clears his throat noisily.

Did I miss something? Are Frank and Roz a
team? Do they have a business arrangement? Jesus,
when did that happen? If so, I have to say that Frank is
not exactly over the moon about it.

'Is that why the bin is so full?' asks Julius. 'Have
you started clearing out? Someone needs to attend to it.
There's rubbish piled high, and the lid won't close.'

Bloody hell, Julius, I'm thinking, why don't you
man up and do something physical for a change? That
saying, *the pen is mightier than the sword*, definitely
doesn't apply to you. Just get on and do something
useful. Like attending to the bins. That would be a start,
right there.

I grab a trash bag and make for the bins. The
recycle bin is twice the size of the normal bin and
always empty, apart from food packaging and Roz's
wine bottles. I'm contemplating simply moving stuff
from the small bin into the recycle bin, but I think better
of it. The last thing I want before a holiday weekend is
a stoush with the bin men. They can be surprisingly
principled and stubborn when it comes to trash. And
they are always built like rugby players. I reach in and

grab what's on top. It looks clean enough: old photographs, chiefly of Frank's mother, by the look, coat hangers, an old blanket (I lift this out carefully) and a prodigious amount of clothing, including Frank's floral shirt. I fill up the bag and shut the lid on the bin. And then, on a whim (I haven't stolen anything for over a week), I grab the shirt. It's an okay shirt, I'm thinking. It's not a good look on Frank, but it will look perfect on me. I think Meg will like me in it.

Of course, I'll have to wait until Frank and Roz have moved out. By that time, Julius will have reconciled with Poppy. It will just be Meg and me. Meg and me. Megme. Meegme. Meegmee.

Bliss.

CHAPTER TWENTY-SIX

THURSDAY 9th APRIL

The police came today with a search warrant. Just like that. It's as if finding Chelsea's body has set them off.

Roz has just finished writing on the whiteboard. Twenty-nine new cases, down from fifty yesterday, and fifty-four the day before, bringing the total number of cases in our country to 1239. This is a mere drop in the bucket compared to numbers worldwide. It is a cause for celebration, and Roz has a smile on her face. Julius is in the kitchen watching her, and they elbow-bump.

The Prime Minister has made a speech on TV and addressed it to the nation: "In the face of the greatest threat to human health that we have faced in over a century, Kiwis have quietly and collectively implemented a nationwide wall of defence. You are breaking the chain of transmission, and you did it for each other." It's a feel-good speech. And you can see that Jacinda is in the mood to party (socially distancing, of course) because she's gone for her glossy-long-hair look. She really has great hair and a beautiful smile. You can sense the spirit of the New Zealand *team of five million* lifting all across the country.

And then the police arrive. It is the same two officers. They don't bother knocking on the front door, as they did last time. They come straight round the back and yell through the door.

'Police! Police!' they shout. 'Open up!'

Meg comes out of her room when they arrive. Except it isn't Meg anymore. Gone is the two-piece and the diaphanous wrap. She's wearing a long skirt and a high-necked blouse. And she has scraped her hair back into a tight ponytail (not your best look, Meg; someone needs to tell you this). And she isn't wearing any make-up, not that she needs make-up; she has a beautiful complexion, but every girl looks sexier with lip gloss and mascara, right? She looks a lot older, almost matronly.

And then she goes to the back door and opens it as if she owns the place.

'Liz, you all right?' says the taller of the two, Sergeant Chambers.

'Yes, sir,' answers Meg. 'All under control.'

I am not sure if I heard this right. I'm actually finding it hard to concentrate. There seem to be not two, but three strangers here. Meg, what is your name? How can you be Liz after you've been Meg? My Meg. There's a thumping in my head, and I'm feeling like someone else as well.

But the truly amazing thing is that Meg doesn't sound like Meg anymore. She has lost her posh accent. She sounds like Roz, a bit nasal and definitely not British. She won't look at me.

And now everyone has assembled in the kitchen, and Sergeant Chambers is pulling something from his jacket pocket.

'Leo Murdoch,' he announces officiously, 'I have a warrant to search your property here at Oak Tree Lodge, including all guest rooms and out-house buildings. I would like your co-operation. And that of everyone else,' he adds, looking at each of us in turn. He has kept his hat on, not like last time, when he took it off and tucked it under his arm.

'You can't come in here,' says Roz.

'I'm sorry, Miss, but we're just doing our job.'

'Your job is to keep everyone safe. That's your job.'

'That's exactly what we're trying to do.'

'You've already interviewed us and searched the house,' I say.

'Officer, may I ask what you are looking for?' asks Julius.

'We're investigating the murder of Chelsea Green.'

'We've already answered all your questions,' I say.

'This is no longer a missing-person investigation, Mr Murdoch. It's now a homicide. I'm sorry for the inconvenience. We will observe social distancing protocols. Perhaps everyone could simply wait in the garden.'

Without a word, Roz heads for the door that leads out of the kitchen, and I can hear her walking up the hallway. The front door bangs, and then she has made her way into the back garden. She's lighting a cigarette and pacing by the back fence.

'We need to check all the rooms,' says Constable Banks reasonably. 'We'll be as quick as we can, but we ask for your co-operation.'

'Certainly,' I say. 'You've got it.'

What choice do I have? Let them poke around as long as they want. It's a good thing I got rid of Chelsea's panties and bra and shoes. After the close call with Prince and Meg, I tossed them into a public bin. They'll have to come back another day to search the shed because I won't be handing over the key.

'We'll start at the front,' says the constable, and, with that, they make for the hall. Meg follows them and leads them into her room. And then the door closes, and I can hear their muffled voices. Meg is doing most of the talking, and within a few minutes, they have come out again. Meg has stayed in her room and shut the door. I guess she's social distancing.

Frank's room is next. He's left his door wide-open as if to say, *welcome, come right in: I've got nothing to hide.* Not only that, he's gone out. He's trying to convey a message. *I've got better things to do than worry about your silly games, officers.*

Just as well Frank's had a tidy-up. Oak Tree Lodge is a reputable establishment, and Frank definitely lowers the tone. I just hope he did some cleaning as well. I really don't want the police putting it about that the lodgers at Oak Tree are filthy.

Frank must have done a reasonable cull because the police are in and out within ten minutes. They spend a good portion of that time checking out Frank's piano. I hear the lid go up, and a tune played. How thorough is a ten-minute search, I'm thinking.

This leaves Julius. And me, of course. Julius is hovering. He stands in the doorway and watches the police as they enter his room. It's surprisingly cluttered with books and notebooks and ring-binders and newspapers. There are also a lot of photos of Poppy on the bedside table. He's even mounted a black-and-white shot of Poppy and himself above the bed. Julius didn't ask permission to punch a hole in the wall. I'll need to speak to him about that. He really is an arrogant prick.

'You are taking a lot of interest in the murder cases, sir,' says Constable Banks. 'Is there a reason for that?'

'I'm doing a journalism course, so I'm studying the writing, you know, the reporting.'

'Journalists write about other things. The coronavirus, for example,' says Sergeant Chambers.

'Well, yes, but these recent homicides are interesting, you have to admit,' says Julius.

'Mmm. How so?'

'Well, the girls have all been found near here. So, naturally, I'm interested.'

'I see,' says the sergeant in exactly that tone that tells me his antennae are fully extended.

'Look, mate, I can't go to Uni in lockdown, so I've got an assignment to do at home. I'm supposed to write something about what is current, you know, what is touching people's lives.'

'I see,' repeats the sergeant.

'And you'd have to say that The Graveyard Ripper is pretty much front and centre of what's topical right now, you know, what people want to read about. I'm just trying to get my assignment done,' wheedles Julius.

They spend over an hour in Julius's room. It's his own fault. If he'd been more casual, they wouldn't have gone through every ring binder and notebook. And he's got newspapers that refer to the murder of Janet Lane and Molly Bell laid out on his bed. I can see that he has highlighted certain paragraphs on the front pages. In pink. Not a good look, Julius.

And now it's my turn. I'm wondering why they left me till last. I guess it figures. My apartment is upstairs. I can't help noticing they've missed the bathroom. A bit of a relief, really. I would prefer that they didn't discover my peep-hole. That would be a downer. Meg would probably draw all the wrong conclusions. Things are already fraught around here. All the upheaval is obviously getting to her. She's become a totally different person. She doesn't seem to know her own name. Or maybe she does, and she gave me a false name in the first place. I really need to sort this out.

The police spend even longer checking out my digs. I decide to wait it out downstairs. I don't want to appear anxious. But, I have to admit, I'm not exactly calm. It's hard to be chill when someone is rooting around your stuff. I can hear drawers being pulled out and kitchen cupboards opening and closing. I can also hear the bed being shifted. I don't think they did that in the other rooms. I'm thinking of Edith, my cleaning lady, and when this area was last cleaned.

They're also spending time in my wardrobe. I can tell because the floorboards creak in there. It's a weird space, dark with a sloping ceiling. It invites suspicion. It's a perfect hiding place, and the plods are giving it a good going over. Over time I have stored a lot of things in there that are best described as sex aids. They're what you buy on the internet and have delivered by courier in a brown package to your door. That's if you lack the courage to just front in the porn shop at the back of the arcade and spend time browsing the shelves, making nice with all the nutters who visit.

Anyway, there's nothing there. Not just at the minute. I find I get bored with things quite quickly, so there's a high turnover. Stimulation and excitement come at a high price. Most of what I consider past its use-by-date, I simply store in the shed or get rid of. I chucked Chelsea's stuff because it was no longer a good vibe. Not after the close call I had with Meg. It almost ruined everything between Meg and me. I don't think she would have understood if she'd come across another girl's underwear in my wardrobe.

Finally, Chambers and Banks come down the stairs. I notice they take their time with this. Constable Banks has a good look at the photograph of "my parents" on the landing. This man obviously has a soft side. I hope he accepts with good grace the fact that I've mislaid the key to the shed and doesn't make a fuss.

'So you like looking at paintings of naked women?' asks Sergeant Chambers. Of course, he's referring to the Botticelli painting opposite my bed. This is not really a question. It comes across as a threat, an attack on my character.

'I enjoy art,' I say.

'Oh, yeah?' he replies.

'Yes, it's a painting of the birth of Venus, you know, when she rose from a shell. It's considered to be a masterpiece,' I say with some authority. 'It was painted in the sixteenth century,' I add.

But the sergeant is not listening. 'We'll be needing the key to the shed,' he says.

'I don't know where it is. I can't remember when I last went in there,' I say.

'Fine,' says Chambers. 'Have it your way.'

K. F. FLEMING

CHAPTER TWENTY-SEVEN

The police waste no time in breaking in. They don't smash the door down. You see that in a lot of movies, don't you? The heaving assault of the burly rescuer until the timber splits. Instead, Constable Banks pulls something from his pocket and has the padlock open in a jiffy. I'll have to get the lowdown on that sometime. It could come in handy.

And now they have yanked open the door, which is quite stiff and catches on the concrete floor. It's dark inside the shed. There is a light switch, but it's behind the door, and you would have to know where to look. So Banks and Chambers linger in the entranceway, trying to adjust to the gloom against the bright sunshine.

I'm very tidy and well-organised, and so the contents of the shed are carefully arranged on the floor-to-ceiling shelves that I had specially made. Everything has been stacked in chronological order, the polar opposite of the way food is displayed in supermarkets, with the old food at the front and the fresh produce out of sight at the back. So, for example, the hat from the chemist is right at the front. And right next to it are things that belonged to Chelsea. Further back is stuff that I acquired before lockdown. And these items are mixed in with things that have accumulated in the eight years since I've been at Oak Tree Lodge.

Roz has overcome her terror of the virus to come away from the back fence. Curiosity is a powerful force.

But she's scared, and there is a civil war being waged within her. Her face is a picture of torment, but she's made her decision. She would rather die than miss the show.

And now Julius is joining her with a positive spring in his step. He is carrying his clipboard and has tucked his pen behind his right ear. Jesus. What is wrong with these people? They remind me of the rubberneckers, first on the scene of a pile-up, hell-bent on photographing the carnage.

I'm thinking I might leave the police to it when Chambers steps out of the shed and calls me over.

'What is all this?' he asks. He's holding up a bright green sleeveless top and a pair of jeans with the knees cut out.

'That's Chelsea's top,' says Roz. 'I recognise it. She always looked good in that top. And I'm pretty sure those are her jeans. I never liked them.'

I really can't wait for Roz to move out. It can't come soon enough.

'People leave stuff behind when they check out sometimes. Quite often, actually: you would be amazed,' I say. 'I keep it in case they come back, you know, store it. It's a kind of lost and found area. It's just a service I provide here at Oak Tree Lodge. There's nothing worse than someone returning for something they left behind only to be told that you tossed it out.'

'You really have your fair share of careless guests,' says Chambers.

'No more than anyone else, I wouldn't think,' I say. 'Guests are usually quite stressed on moving out day. And anxiety tends to make one forgetful.'

'Quite the little psychologist, aren't you?' says Banks. I guess I misread him when he was looking at the portrait on the landing. He really is a nasty man with unkind, narrow lips. A bit like Frank when I think about it.

'How come so much of this stuff is new?' asks Chambers.

'Search me,' I reply.

'That's what we intend to do,' says Banks in a belligerent tone.

'Who leaves behind a brand-new negligee? Look, the tag is still attached,' says Chambers, holding up a flimsy piece of white silk and lace.

I must admit I'm a bit distracted by the garment and my memory of the day I took it. And the fun I had upstairs as I tried it on with my best boots. So I don't say anything.

'And these?' pesters Chambers. He has scooped up a rather fetching flesh-coloured bra and matching panties and is brandishing them between his right thumb and forefinger.

'How should I know?' I say. I turn to look at Roz, who has obviously forgotten all about the coronavirus because she has now moved to a position right by the door of the shed, within inches of Chambers. She has rolled her sleeves up, and her eyebrows are high. I've never seen anyone so amped.

Julius has moved closer too and has taken on a journalistic pose: side-on to the shed and leaning into his clipboard. He is writing furiously. Does he think I'm The Graveyard Ripper? And he's got the scoop? Julius, the only column you'll ever be writing will be a gossip column for bored housewives. Or maybe, if you work your way up through the ranks, you'll be let loose on horoscopes.

'Wow!' says Roz.

'And who leaves a dress behind?' asks Chambers, displaying a mid-calf, black garment with long sleeves.

'Looks expensive,' says Roz.

Roz is not often right, but she is in this case. The price tag tells the story. It really is a beautiful dress, silk. I couldn't resist it. Actually, it looked good on me. It didn't go with the boots, though.

'Look, officer, I really don't know the answer to why girls leave stuff behind. I'm not a mind-reader,' I say. And now Banks is taking the dress from Chambers and turning it over in his hands. Jesus, these guys are complete perverts, getting off on this stuff.

'I think you've answered my questions, sir,' says Chambers.

I wait for what is coming.

'It's all women's clothing. There's nothing here belonging to a man. Nothing at all. Don't you find that strange? That only girls feel anxiety and forget things, never men?'

'Well, actually,' I begin, but Chambers has obviously made a decision. He makes some sort of sign to Banks, who leaves the shed and walks around the side of the house.

Roz steps away to let him past and then moves back into position as if she's saving her place in the queue for the Moscow Circus. It's really hot out here in the garden, and I'm beginning to overheat. I'm overdressed as usual (I blame Meg for this), and there is sweat rolling down my spine. Frank's floral shirt would be a whole lot cooler than this linen fabric, but I'm going to have to wait for that. I've actually stored it in the shed, at the front, unfortunately (latest addition), but at least it's partially out of sight, obscured behind the open door.

Banks is back. He's carrying three large plastic bags, and he's wearing gloves. He hands a pair of gloves to Chambers. It's too late for that, I'm thinking. Isn't the evidence already well and truly *contaminated*, as they say in all the forensic file programmes you see on TV?

Chambers has snatched up the silk dress (careful with that) and underwear and is stuffing them into one of the bags. And now he has the floral shirt. He's not sure about this item. Maybe it's not thrilling enough for him. It's too figure-concealing, and he's wondering if there's any upside to taking it. I can just imagine the field day these law enforcement officers will have when they get back to the station. And the floral shirt won't cut it. They take it anyway. I guess it would give the game away if they just confiscated the sexy stuff.

I don't think either Roz or Julius noticed the shirt go into the bag. Julius was too busy writing, and Roz was feeling around for her cigarettes. Thank God. Maybe she'll take herself off and blow smoke on her herb garden instead of up her arse. It was a relief that they didn't see Frank's shirt. Imagine what they would have thought. Especially Julius: *Poor old Leo has to root around in his own trash bin for clothing, like the homeless people in the arcade.*

It's getting unbearably hot out here, and I need to get myself in the shade. But I also need to wait it out. I need to know how much of my stuff these guys take. That's only reasonable, to want to see what's being taken from you. It's a bit like a stock take in reverse.

To cut a long story short, Sergeant Chambers and Constable Banks make a meal of it. They grab absolutely everything. Apart from the hat. They have no interest in the hat, even though it's the most recent robbery and still has the tag attached as plain as day. I guess it's just not very raunchy.

And now they are asking me to accompany them to the station. I must admit, I'm taken aback by this. How can they have more questions? I've told them everything. I've got stuff in my shed. So what? It proves nothing. Maybe some of it looks a little dodgy. Maybe I've done some shoplifting. In the overall scheme of things, it's hardly The Great Train Robbery. A bit of petty pilfering never hurt anybody. Surely these guys have more important things to do, like saving more girls from being murdered in the streets. And what about the coronavirus? Shouldn't they be checking that everyone is sticking to the protocols? Priorities. It's all about priorities in life. Police, of all people, should understand this.

I decide to say nothing more. Isn't that what the lawyers tell you? Volunteer nothing. Simply answer questions as briefly as possible. So I'm going with them. It's only a five-minute ride downtown to the station. That's one of the advantages of living in the inner city. Everything's right here, on-hand. I must admit, it's nice being driven. Chambers sits in the back with me, and Banks drives, my chauffeur. It's a good feeling.

'Am I under arrest?' I ask as I walk into the police station.

This question is ignored, and I can't help being a little put out. What's that Latin phrase? Quid pro quo. The Romans understood the principle of give and take. They were a civilised lot. I've been good enough to answer all their questions. And now they won't even answer one of mine.

They usher me into a small room with a large internal window, which looks out into the hallway. I can see people coming and going. Just as well Roz isn't joining us, I'm thinking. It really is very crowded in here with Chambers and Banks. The dimensions of the room make social distancing impossible. In fact, I think I'm only about two feet away from these policemen, who spend their days walking the streets and rubbing shoulders with all manner of criminals. This is the perfect incubator for the coronavirus: a kind of giant petri dish. They are sitting across the cheap wooden desk from me. Banks has a notebook and pen. I guess that means Chambers will be chief interrogator, and Banks will play secretary.

They turn on a recording device.

'You're not under arrest, Mr Murdoch, but you are here under suspicion of the murder of Chelsea Green,' says Chambers.

And then, before I have time to answer, he puts the question directly to me.

'Did you murder Chelsea Green?'

I realise I don't have to say anything at all and can just plead my Miranda rights or whatever they're called. But I also realise that this would simply make me look guilty. I decide to answer their crazy questions.

'No, I did not,' I say.

'What do you know about the murder of Chelsea Green?'

'I don't know anything about the murder of Chelsea Green. I didn't even know she was dead until I read the article in the newspaper yesterday.'

'But you knew she was missing.'

'Not exactly.' I'm thinking I wish I had taken a diazepam before I left.

'What do you mean?' asks Chambers. He is sweating. Good.

'She left Oak Tree Lodge without saying she was going; that's all I know.'

'She also left without taking her stuff. It's all there in your shed, Mr Murdoch. Why would that be?'

'Like I said, I don't like to throw things away.'

'Why not?'

'It's a waste.'

'What good is it to you?'

'Look, I'm a fair-minded citizen. I'm just storing it for her, you know, keeping it in case she comes back.'

'A sort of Lost and Found?'

'Yes, I've already explained all this. Look, officer, I don't like where this is going. Chelsea left some things behind. Not all her things. Isn't that the important point? She didn't leave everything behind. She took some stuff with her, the essential stuff. And what she did leave, I've stored for her. How can that be a crime? So now I'm being punished for being a responsible, caring landlord?'

'Mr Murdoch, how do you explain that she left behind her cat? Her cat, Prince, which by all accounts she adored?'

'How do you know that?'

'Are you denying it?'

'No, I'm asking how you know that.'

'We have a witness.'

'Quentin. Quentin Adams. He's completely crazy; you know that, don't you?'

'So you maintain that you know nothing about the disappearance of Chelsea Green,' says Chambers, leaning forward. He's way too close, and I am feeling a bit like Roz at this point. Honestly, I might as well plead guilty because he's killing me with Covid-19. I'm probably already the walking dead.

'I do, yes,' I say. And at that moment, I see Meg (Liz) through the window. She is wearing a police uniform, and her hair is pinned up in a bun. She looks a bit like Roz. I get only a glimpse, but I notice the wedding ring on her finger as she reaches up to tuck in a strand of her hair that has come loose.

I don't know exactly what happened next. I must admit I lost focus on what was going on in the room, but I am being set free. Constable Banks drives me home. He doesn't speak to me. I'm glad of this because I'm feeling light-headed and, actually, if I'm honest, completely out-of-control. Mr Mad is talking to me and making perfect sense.

It's not a good vibe.

K. F. FLEMING

CHAPTER TWENTY-EIGHT

SUNDAY 12th APRIL

It's Easter, Easter Sunday. Everything is quiet. Churches are shut: there are no services, and parishioners have to stay at home. Zoom has become a thing. People do video conferencing, and some churches are offering services online. As an essential worker, the Easter Bunny is doing the rounds, but that's pretty much it. Kids are conducting their egg hunts in their own backyards and searching for bears in windows. No-one's allowed to go to the beach or visit their holiday homes.

It's like a funeral parlour at Oak Tree. Frank is keeping to his room. Roz spends the day in the garden talking to her herbs and watering her yucca. And Julius is on his phone the whole time. That's when he's not closeted in his room, no doubt labouring over his treatise that will never see the light of day. They all think I've got something to do with the disappearance of Chelsea. I can see it in their faces. They also think I'm involved in the death of Molly Bell. They won't talk to me. They ignore me.

Let them. Bring it on. I'm glad of the silence. It's peaceful, not having to watch Roz reciting the latest coronavirus statistics and washing the lettuce.

The only thing I'm not glad of is the emptiness of Room One. Liz (I have to start calling Meg Liz; that's her name, after all) has gone. She must have packed up her things and left when the police were searching the shed and asking their useless questions. I miss her. I spend a lot of time upstairs in my bedroom looking out over the garden, imagining her in her two-piece. A vision of loveliness in my garden: that's what you were, Liz. A babe, my babe. But not just beauty. You had discernment and taste. You got me. Not like that Chelsea, who really had no idea. Honestly, you could have put Michelangelo's statue of David right in front of her, and she would have had no idea what she was looking at. Self-sabotage, that was Chelsea Green's problem. She didn't know when she was onto a good thing. Nobody's fault. Certainly not mine. Inevitable.

I forgive you, Liz. You were only doing your job. It must have been so hard for you. Your mission was to spy on me, investigate me. You didn't have a choice. It was the assignment from hell, and your superiors had no business laying it on you. That man you went off with in the car. He was another plod. I see that now. You had no choice. You couldn't even finish your shower.

Mission Impossible: that's what it was. You did your best. How could you possibly have known that you would fall in love with me? None of that is in the police manuals, I bet. You were supposed to be a honey trap. Well, you succeeded. Well and truly. But you got caught up in your own honey. And now we are stuck. Honey, it's the nectar of the gods. Divine: that is exactly the right word to describe our relationship.

When this is all over, when they finally catch The Graveyard Ripper, I'll come, see you, and we'll pick up where we left off. The pandemic will be under control by then. We will be able to go wherever we want, Liz-Meg. I will show you the best time any girl could ever dream of. I'm counting the days. This is day eighteen. Not long to go. The police will have their man by then. Of course, Easter will probably be holding things up a little, but I can wait. I'm not going anywhere. And Oak Tree will be much better when Frank has moved out and taken his smell with him. Roz too. I'll get younger people in, but not too young. Not like Julius. I don't want testosterone-loaded males marking out their patch on my territory. I'll take it slowly, choose wisely so that you have some stimulating, intelligent company.

I say nothing is happening at Oak Tree, but something truly shocking has happened today.

Sergeant Chambers and Constable Banks show up again. I am in the garden, actually in the shed with the hat, when they come. They must have tried the front door first and then come around the back. They stand outside the door, peering into the gloom. They insist that I go with them to the station.

I tell them I have nothing further to add to my previous testimony and that they are wasting their time. I also suggest that they turn their attention to Quentin Adams.

'It's always the husband or boyfriend,' I say. You would think they must know this.

'We are following several lines of enquiry,' says Chambers, who, I must say, is very versed in the art of police-speak.

'What?' I ask.

'We're interested in the murder of Molly Bell,' he replies.

I think I must have misheard him. And so I ask him to repeat what he has said, and then I can't help thinking he is very disrespectful because he is shouting at me as if I was deaf or something.

And then, stupidly, I say, 'What about Chelsea Green?'

They don't reply to that. Instead, they explain to me that I have the right to remain silent. I know at this point that things must be serious, and I decide not to say anything. I don't have a lawyer, but it's looking as though I may need one.

So here I am in the same poky police-station interview room, where the coronavirus doesn't seem to matter.

Sergeant Chambers is doing the talking again, and Constable Banks is on paperwork.

'What do you know about Molly Bell?' asks Chambers.

I decided I might as well answer their pointless questions.

'Even less than I know about Chelsea Green,' I say. 'I never met the girl.'

'And yet you went to look at her place of death in the graveyard,' says Chambers.

'I did. But it wasn't my idea. I went there with my girlfriend. It was her idea. She said she had always been fascinated by crime and what motivated people to kill. She said she wanted to see the scene of the crime. And besides, we weren't the only ones there. Lots of people gathered in the graveyard to pay their respects. There were flowers and candles and prayers, a bit like when Princess Diana died.'

'So you didn't go there to revisit the scene, to relive the thrill of murdering an innocent young girl?'

I know exactly what they're doing with this confronting question, and I don't take the bait. I open my arms wide to show that I'm letting them in, and I'm being frank and open and honest (I've read about how the police study body language and draw conclusions from folded arms or lack of eye contact or whatever) and I say, 'I can assure you, officers, I went there that day with my girlfriend. It was a date.' I feel good saying this. I bet neither of these clowns has girlfriends.

And then Chambers goes in for the kill. 'How do you account for the fact that there are traces of Molly Bell's DNA on some of the clothing we took from your shed?' he asks, with a very unflattering curl of his top lip.

'That's impossible,' I say.

'I can assure you, it is possible because it's a fact,' says Chambers.

'I can't account for it,' I say. 'There is no possible explanation. There must be some mistake. Maybe someone planted the evidence, or there's been some contamination. It often happens.'

Chambers and Banks eye me silently.

'Look, there has to be a mix-up. You guys must have messed up. I notice you didn't put any gloves on until the last minute,' I say.

There really should be a window in this cramped room. It's all starting to smell a bit like Frank.

'Would you consent to our taking a blood sample?' asks Chambers.

I'm thinking I need to consider this. I don't want to provide them with my DNA, but I don't want to come across as obstructive. I take my time pondering my options and eventually decide I have nothing to lose.

In the end, they simply take a swab. They stick a cotton bud into my mouth, wiggle it around and then secure it in a tube. I guess this is what's happening all over the world. Buds are being shoved into thousands of people every day to test for the coronavirus. Of course, I'm being tested for something different: the Mr Mad gene.

And then they ask if I would mind being fingerprinted.

'Fine, fine,' I say. 'And then I can go?' I ask.

It's all over in minutes, and I am driven back home.

'We'll be in touch,' says Sergeant Chambers. 'Don't go anywhere,' he adds ominously as if I'm guilty and a flight risk. What planet are these goons on? I couldn't go anywhere if I wanted to.

Roz is at the whiteboard doing her updates: eighteen new cases, down from twenty-nine yesterday and forty-four the day before, bringing the total number of cases to 1330. The whole country is proud. Our Prime Minister is repeating her mantra (one of her many): "You are breaking the chain of transmission, and you did it for each other." Jacinda has become the mother of the nation. We are all her children, doing what we are told and basking in her positive reinforcement.

'What happened?' Roz asks, handing me the sanitiser. Her hair has come adrift, and she looks a mess. Her sleeves are rolled up well past her elbows, and I notice that she hasn't done up the buttons of her blouse properly, so that there is a flap of fabric at the bottom and a bunch at the top.

Julius has walked into the room. To what do I owe this welcoming committee, I'm thinking. Jesus, I've become the floorshow in my own home. Roz and Julius can't wait to see the next Act.

'Where's Frank?' I ask.

'He's packing,' says Roz.

I decide to come clean. I might as well get it over with.

'The police seem to have the crazy idea that I have something to do with the death of Molly Bell. Apparently, they have found her blood or whatever on some of my clothes.'

'So what about Chelsea? Do they think you had nothing to do with her death?' asks Julius. He sounds disappointed as if the curtain is coming down on the show he has been waiting all morning to see. Who needs enemies when you've got lodgers like Julius, I'm thinking.

'That's right, Julius,' I say.

'So why do they think you have anything to do with Molly Bell? You don't even know her,' says Julius. He's trying to make this last sentence a statement, but actually, I can tell it's a question because his voice goes up at the end.

'They think they've got evidence. It's all bullshit,' I say. 'It's totally insane.'

And now Roz has put the marker pen back on the ledge of the whiteboard and is walking to the dining room table. She's a little unsteady on her feet and grips the side of the table as she collapses into the captain's chair.

'It's not insane,' says Roz.

'Well, thank you very much for that vote of confidence, Roz. I'll remember you in my will when they shove the needle in,' I say.

'The police have got Frank's shirt, haven't they?' she says.

'No,' I say. I really don't want to own up to this. I don't think it puts me in a very good light. Scavenging second-hand clothing from bins is not really how I want to be remembered.

'Look, Leo, I saw the police take the clothing from the shed. And I saw them take that floral shirt of Frank's,' says Roz. Her eyes are bloodshot, and I notice she's forgotten her mascara. 'I don't need to know how you came by it, how you came by any of it for that matter. It's none of my business. But amongst all the clothing is that shirt.'

'So what?' I ask. I really want to change the subject. Julius is looking at me as if I'm a complete sicko.

'That shirt is dodgy,' says Roz. And now she is making her way to the sink and pouring herself a glass of water. She comes back to the table and lowers herself slowly into the chair. 'Frank hardly ever wore it. It was like he was saving it up for special occasions.'

'Yes?' says Julius.

'I'm so sorry,' says Roz, taking a gulp of water. 'I should have done something, but somehow I didn't. I suspected Frank of something, but I wasn't sure what. He was always so secretive. I would hear him going out late at night and coming home in the small hours. He always crept around and made sure to open and close doors so quietly. And he walked so silently on those feather feet of his. But I could hear him. I could always hear him. Oh, God!' Roz's voice has started to tremble, and she lets out a sob.

'Take your time, Roz,' says Julius.

Roz takes a deep breath. 'And he would wear that shirt and play the piano on those days he was going out. Not every day.' Roz pauses and takes another gulp of water. 'Not every day,' she repeats. 'Just sometimes and those times, heaven help me, oh God, those times, those times, well, they coincided with the deaths of Janet Lane and Molly Bell.'

Roz is sobbing again and wipes her face on her forearm. 'And I always thought it odd that he would wear the shirt only once and then wash it straight away when he hardly ever washed anything. Oh, God.'

'Take your time, Roz,' says Julius again.

I wish Julius would shut up with his false empathy. At least he's not taking notes for once.

'I knew for certain that I was right last Sunday when I offered to wash his shirt,' continues Roz, staring down at her hands. 'There was blood on it, and I had to rewash it. So I confronted him. He got defensive. And, of course, his mother had just died, and he offered me some money if I would keep my suspicions to myself. He said, if anything happened to him, I wouldn't get anything.' Roz lets the seconds pass as if she is afraid of what she is about to say. She notices the buttons on her blouse and takes her time fixing them. And then she gathers herself up.

'And so I decided to keep quiet,' she whispers finally.

'So what has changed your mind?' I ask. I don't know why I bother to ask this question when what I should be doing is reading Roz the Riot Act and insisting she phones the police.

'Frank is not going to make good on his promise. He said he would give me money but now he won't. He said he was in the clear now and that you could take the rap.'

What the fuck? That's very noble of you, Roz. You're quite the martyr, putting yourself out for me like this. Selfless and brave. But, actually, you're not fooling anyone, least of all me. This is naked vengeance on

Frank and nothing about doing the right thing by me. I want to scream these words at her, but I don't. I don't say anything at all. I'm going to need Roz. So I say nothing at all.

'But it's not just that,' says Roz hastily, pulling at her sleeves. 'When I started to think about Molly Bell and that poor little girl, who has to go through life without her mum, I couldn't bear it. I just couldn't bear it. That poor, poor little girl. Frank is a monster.'

Roz lets out a cry, and she runs down the hall into her bedroom.

What the fuck, Roz? So you weren't motivated by justice? You didn't for one nanosecond think about me rotting in gaol for someone else's crimes? What the fuck is wrong with you? What were you thinking? Were you even thinking? It must be difficult to hold a rational thought when you drink so much and talk to parsley all day.

And now Mr Mad is putting in an appearance. He's mad as hell. And he's sitting heavy on my shoulder, whispering bad things in my ear. I try not to listen. But he's very insistent, and I'm finding it hard to ignore him.

CHAPTER TWENTY-NINE

OUT OF LOCKDOWN

Frank has been arrested. The police believed Roz's story. She went straight to the police station from here. She ran all the way. She said later that she didn't feel safe at Oak Tree Lodge anymore with Frank sleeping in the room next door to hers.

Frank couldn't deny that he owned the floral shirt. There were too many witnesses willing to testify to that. Ozzy came forward and told the police what he knew. He said he was happy to help me, that I was one of the few people around here who treated him as a human being. And the police interviewed all the girls from Lollipops, as well as the owner and chefs and bartenders. They were keen to co-operate. Janet Lane and Molly Bell had been their friends, after all. And Chelsea. Everyone loved Chelsea. They were glad the killer had been nailed. The relief was overwhelming.

What I don't understand is how forensics managed to lift anything off that shirt, let alone Molly Bell's DNA. It doesn't say much about Roz's laundering skills. Just as well, really. I'm no longer a suspect, and it's all down to Roz's fuck-up. I suppose I should be grateful to her. I'm in the clear. It's a nice feeling, liberating.

The police want to link the murders of Chelsea Green, Janet Lane and Molly Bell. They are hell-bent on this. I can't see the point. Frank will get a life sentence for Molly. Where's the logic in three life sentences? I suppose it gets rid of a huge headache for the police. But, of course, they have to prove it. And they haven't as yet. Frank hasn't confessed. He's maintaining his innocence. Good luck with that. I hope someone in prison has an iPod or something with "As Time Goes By" on the playlist. Frank will need it.

The newspapers have made a meal out of it. "Graveyard Ripper Caught" is the front-page headline day after day. Trial by media. You hear about that, don't you? When there's nothing happening to write about because no-one is being robbed in a pub, killed on the roads or drowned in a boating accident, the Ripper murders are a godsend to the desperate journos. Frank has no chance against all that.

The police paid another visit to Oak Tree Lodge. They had a proper look in Frank's room this time, not a boy-look, which never uncovers anything. They wore gloves and were falling over themselves to be nice as pie to me. Especially Sergeant Chambers, who was positively deferential.

The upside of this is that they are no longer interested in any of the stuff in the shed. It's pretty obvious that I've stolen most of it, but they don't seem interested in pursuing it. They are so euphoric at having caught the Graveyard Ripper that everything else has been eclipsed.

They returned all my stuff three days after the arrest of Frank. Not the shirt, of course. I guess that's their star piece of evidence. Chambers has been interviewed multiple times on prime-time television. He comes across as all community-minded and *just happy to have got a killer off the streets*, but you can see the dimples in his cheeks forming as he basks in his celebrity status and the prospect of a new badge or whatever it is they bestow on promoted cops.

I'm pleased to have it all behind me. Oak Tree has invited some unwelcome attention since all this went down. I'm hoping things will settle, and I can just get on with my life.

Julius is still here. He finished his assignment and got an A pass. He has reconciled with Poppy, and they are going to get married now that lockdown is ended. I feel sorry for Poppy.

Roz is very relieved. She was up for the quite serious charges of accessory after the fact and withholding vital information. But she must have somehow got immunity in exchange for her testimony. She's not as stupid as she looks, that woman. She knows, for example, the power of the quid pro quo.

Now that lockdown has ended, I am going to ask her to leave.

I'm planning on asking Liz out on a date. This time everything will go perfectly. It wasn't her fault that she was sent to Oak Tree to spy on me. She was only doing her job. She had no choice. And, of course, what must have made it intolerable for her was falling in love with her quarry. She was sent to trap me but ended up stuck fast in her own trap.

I'm going to have to get used to her new name. Liz. It's actually okay. It fits. Liz and Leo. It's very couplish. We will be the perfect pair, the dream team. Things will go much better this time.

I've come a long way during lockdown. It's been a whole learning experience. For both of us. I understand where you're coming from, Liz. I saw your wedding ring at the police station. Don't think I didn't notice it. You wanted to show me that you're off-limits to everyone else. That you've saved yourself for me until things have calmed down. I love you for that. Girls who put themselves about are not my type at all.

I forgive you for lying to me and making things up. I know now why you had two phones, one for you and a secret burner phone for official duties. I'm prepared to look past all that. I won't even talk about it. We have so many more important things to discuss, like our future together. So I forgive you with all my heart.

Just as long as you play ball.

I don't want you to end up like Chelsea.

THE END

Acknowledgements

The publishers and authors would like to thank Russell Spencer, Matt Vidler, Susan Woodard, Janelle Hope Leonard West, Lianne Bailey-Woodward, Laura Jayne Humphrey and Katie Major for their work, without which this book would not have been possible.

About the Publisher

L.R. Price Publications is dedicated to publishing books by unknown authors.

We use a mixture of both traditional and modern publishing options, to bring our authors' words to the wider world.

We print, publish, distribute and market books in a variety of formats including paper and hardback, electronic books, digital audiobooks and online.

If you are an author interested in getting your book published, or a book retailer interested in selling our books, please contact us.

www.lrpricepublications.com
L.R. Price Publications Ltd,
27 Old Gloucester Street,
London, WC1N 3AX.
020 3051 9572
publishing@lrprice.com